DELORES FOSSEN

KADE

TORONTO NEW YORK LONDON
AMSTERDAM PARIS SYDNEY HAMBURG
STOCKHOLM ATHENS TOKYO MILAN MADRID
PRAGUE WARSAW BUDAPEST AUCKLAND

Recycling programs for this product may not exist in your area.

ISBN-13: 978-0-373-69627-7

KADE

Copyright © 2012 by Delores Fossen

For questions and comments about the quality of this book please contact us at Customer_eCare@Harlequin.ca.

www.Harlequin.com

Printed in U.S.A.

ABOUT THE AUTHOR

Imagine a family tree that includes Texas cowboys, Choctaw and Cherokee Indians, a Louisiana pirate and a Scottish rebel who battled side by side with William Wallace. With ancestors like that, it's easy to understand why *USA TODAY* bestselling author and former air force captain Delores Fossen feels as if she were genetically predisposed to writing romances. Along the way to fulfilling her DNA destiny, Delores married an air force top gun who just happens to be of Viking descent. With all those romantic bases covered, she doesn't have to look too far for inspiration.

Books by Delores Fossen

CAST OF CHARACTERS

Special Agent Kade Ryland—When his undercover assignment at a shady fertility clinic ends, Kade thinks both the job and the hot attraction are finished for him and his undercover partner. But nine months later, he learns they're the parents of a newborn baby girl.

Special Agent Bree Winston—She's a deep-cover operative who considers herself married to the job, but she must risk everything to save Kade and their daughter.

Leah Ryland—Kade and Bree's newborn daughter.

Randy "Coop" Cooper—Bree's boss and mentor, but there are rumors that he's on the take and could be responsible for the danger to Kade and Bree.

Hector McClendon—Former head of the Fulbright Fertility Clinic. He's possibly the man who wants Kade and Bree dead so they can't testify against him at his upcoming trial.

Anthony McClendon—Hector's son, he's under investigation for his part in the illegal practices at his father's fertility clinic.

Jamie Grier—She was a nurse at the now infamous fertility clinic, but she claims she's an innocent woman.

Chapter One

Special Agent Kade Ryland raced up the steps of the Silver Creek hospital. Whatever was going on, it was bad. No doubt about it. The voice message from his brother had proven that.

Get to the hospital now, Grayson had ordered.

Since his brother Grayson was the sheriff of Silver Creek, it couldn't be good news. Nor was the fact that Grayson wasn't answering his phone—probably because he was in the hospital, a dead zone for reception.

Kade prayed that someone wasn't hurt or dead, but the odds were that's exactly what had happened. He had four living brothers, three sisters-in-law, two nephews and a niece. Since all his brothers were in law enforcement and one of his sisters-in-law was pregnant, there were lots of opportunities for things to go wrong.

The automatic doors swished open, and he hurried through, only to set off the metal detector's alarm. Kade mumbled some profanity for the delay. He'd just come from work and was still wearing his sidearm in a shoulder holster concealed beneath his jacket. He also had his backup weapon strapped to his boot. He didn't want to take the time to remove either of them.

The uniformed guard practically jumped from the chair where he was reading a battered copy of the

Silver Creek Ledger. His name was Rowdy Dawkins, a man that Kade had known his whole life. But then Kade could say that about half the town.

"The sheriff's waiting for you in the emergency room," Rowdy said, waving Kade through the metal detector. His expression was somber. His tone dripped with concern.

Oh, man.

Kade didn't even take the time to ask Rowdy for details, though the man no doubt knew what was going on. He didn't just hurry—Kade ran to the E.R. that was at the other end of the building. The hospital wasn't big by anyone's standards, but it seemed to take him an hour to reach the E.R. waiting room.

No sign of his brother or any other family member.

Kade's heart was pounding now, and his mind was coming up with all sorts of bad scenarios. He'd been an FBI agent for seven years, not nearly as long as his brothers had been in law enforcement, but that was more than long enough to fuel the worst sort of details about what could be wrong.

"Your brother's in there with Dr. Mickelson," a nurse volunteered as she pointed the way. She, too, gave him a sympathetic look, which meant he was probably the only person in the whole frickin' town who didn't know what the heck was going on.

Kade mumbled a thank-you to her and hurried into the doctor's office, the first door in the hall just off the waiting room. He tried to brace himself for what he might see, but he hadn't expected to find everything looking so…normal.

Well, almost.

Grayson was indeed there, standing, and looking fit as a fiddle as his granddaddy Chet would have said. He looked as he usually did in his jeans and crisp white shirt with his badge clipped to his rodeo belt.

Dr. Mickelson, the chief of staff, was there, as well, practically elbow to elbow with Grayson. Nothing looked out of the ordinary for him, either. The two had obviously been expecting him.

"I was in the middle of an arrest when you phoned," Kade started. "That's why your call went straight to voice mail, but I tried to get in touch with you after I got your message. I tried your office, too, and the dispatch clerk said her orders were for me to speak directly to you. What's wrong? Who's hurt?"

"No one's hurt," Grayson said, but then he wearily shook his head. "At least no one that we know about." He stepped closer and looked directly into Kade's eyes. Ice-gray eyes that were a genetic copy of Kade's own.

Oh, yeah. This was bad.

And downright confusing.

"What do you mean by that?" Kade asked.

Grayson and the doctor exchanged glances. "You'd better sit down. We have something to tell you." The doctor tipped his head to the chair next to his desk, which was cluttered with folders, computer equipment and papers.

The one thing Kade didn't want was to sit. "Does someone in the family have cancer or something?"

Or God forbid, had there been a suicide? It wasn't something the average person would consider high on their list of worries, but since his own mother had committed suicide when he was barely eleven, it was never far from Kade's mind.

"No one has cancer," the doctor answered. He flexed his graying eyebrows, but he didn't add more.

Like the security guard, Kade knew Dr. Mickelson.

The doctor had been the one to deliver him thirty-one years ago, but Kade couldn't read the doctor as well as he could read Grayson. So, he turned to his brother.

"Tell me what happened," Kade pushed.

Grayson mumbled something under his breath. "I would if I knew where to start."

"The beginning's usually a good place." Kade's stomach was churning now, the acid blistering his throat, and he just wanted to know the truth.

"All right." Grayson took a deep breath and stepped to the side.

Kade saw it then. The clear bassinet on rollers, the kind they used in the hospital nursery.

He walked closer and looked inside. There was a baby, and it was likely a girl since there was a pink blanket snuggled around her. There was also a little pink stretchy cap on her head. She was asleep, but her mouth was puckered as if sucking a bottle.

"What does the baby have to do with this?" Kade asked.

"Everything. Two days ago someone abandoned her in the E.R. waiting room," the doctor explained. "The person left her in an infant carrier next to one of the chairs. We don't know who did that because we don't have security cameras."

Kade was finally able to release the breath he'd been holding. So, this was job-related. They'd called him in because he was an FBI agent.

But he immediately rethought that.

"An abandoned baby isn't a federal case," Kade clarified, though Grayson already knew that. Kade reached down and brushed his index finger over a tiny dark curl that peeked out from beneath the cap. "You think she was kidnapped or something?"

When neither the doctor nor Grayson answered, Kade looked back at them. Anger began to boil through him. "Did someone hurt her?"

"No," the doctor quickly answered. "There wasn't a scratch on her. She's perfectly healthy as far as I can tell."

The anger went as quickly as it'd come. Kade had handled the worst of cases, but the one thing he couldn't stomach was anyone harming a child.

"I called Grayson as soon as she was found," the doctor went on. "There were no Amber Alerts, no reports of missing newborns. There wasn't a note in her carrier, only a bottle that had no prints, no fibers or anything else to distinguish it."

Kade lifted his hands palm up. "That's a lot of *noes*. What do you know about her?" Because he was sure this was leading somewhere.

Dr. Mickelson glanced at the baby. "We know she's about three or four days old, which means she was abandoned either the day she was born or shortly after. She's slightly underweight, barely five pounds, but there was no hospital bracelet. We had no other way to identify her so we ran a DNA test two days ago when she arrived and just got back the results." His explanation stopped cold, and his attention came back to Kade.

So did Grayson's. "Kade, she's yours."

Kade leaned in because he was certain he'd misheard what his brother said. "Excuse me?"

"The baby is your daughter," Grayson clarified.

Because that was the last thing Kade expected to come from his brother's mouth, it took several seconds to sink in. Okay, more than several, and when it finally registered in his brain, it didn't sink in well.

All the air vanished from the room.

"That's impossible," Kade practically shouted.

The baby began to squirm from the noise. Kade's reaction was just as abrupt. What the devil was going on here? He wasn't a father. Heck, he hadn't been in a real relationship in nearly two years.

Grayson groaned and tipped his eyes to the ceiling. "Not impossible according to the DNA."

Kade did some groaning, as well, and would have spit out a denial or two, but the baby started to cry. Grayson looked at Kade as if he expected him to do something, but Kade was too stunned to move. Grayson huffed, reached down, gently scooped her up and began to rock her.

"The DNA test has to be wrong," Kade concluded.

But he stared at that tiny crying face. She did have dark hair, like the Rylands. The shape of her face was familiar, too, similar to his own niece, but all babies looked pretty much the same to him.

"I had the lab run two genetic samples to make sure," the doctor interjected. "And then Grayson put the results through a bunch of databases. Your DNA was already in there."

Yeah. Kade knew his DNA was in the system. Most federal employees were. But that didn't mean the match had been correct.

"Who's the baby's mother?" Kade demanded.

Because whoever she was, all of this wasn't adding up. A baby who just happened to match an FBI agent's DNA.

His DNA.

A bottle with no fingerprints. And the baby had been abandoned at the hospital in his hometown, where his family owned a very successful ranch.

All of that couldn't be a coincidence.

"We don't know the identity of the child's mother," the doctor answered. "We didn't get a database match on the maternal DNA."

And that did even more to convince Kade that this was some kind of setup. But then he rethought that. Most people didn't have their DNA recorded in a law enforcement system unless they'd done something to get it there.

Like break the law.

"Since you haven't mentioned a girlfriend," Grayson continued, "you're probably looking at the result of a one-night stand. Don't bother to tell me you haven't had a few of those."

He had. Kade couldn't deny there had been one or two, but he'd always taken precautions. *Always.* The same as he had in his longer relationships.

"Think back eight to nine months ago," Grayson prompted. "I already checked the calendar you keep on the computer at the ranch, and I know you were on assignments both months."

Kade forced himself to think and do the math. He could dispel this entire notion of the baby being his if he could figure out where he'd been during that critical time. It took some doing, but he picked through the smeared recollections of assignments, reports and briefings.

The nine-month point didn't fit because he'd done surveillance in a van. Alone. But eight and a half months ago he'd been in San Antonio, days into an undercover assignment that involved the Fulbright Fertility Clinic, a facility that was into all sorts of nasty things, including genetic experiments on embryos, questionable surrogates and illegal adoptions.

Kade froze.

"What?" Grayson demanded. "You remembered something?"

Oh, yeah. He remembered *something*.

Kade squeezed his eyes shut a moment. "I teamed up with a female deep-cover agent. A Jane we call them. She already had established ties with someone who worked in the clinic so we partnered up. We posed as a married couple with fertility issues so we could infiltrate the clinic. We were literally locked in the place for four days."

Kade had been on more than a dozen assignments since the Fulbright case, the details of them all bleeding together, but there was one Texas-size detail about that assignment that stood out.

Bree.

The tough-as-nails petite brunette with the olive-green eyes. During those four days they'd worked together, she'd been closemouthed about her personal life. Heck, he knew hardly anything about her, and what he did know could have been part of the facade of a deep-cover agent.

"We didn't have sex," Kade mumbled. Though he had thought about it a time or two. Posing as a married couple, they'd been forced to sleep in the same bed and put on a show of how much they *loved* each other.

"There must be someone else, then," Grayson insisted.

"Alice Marks," Kade admitted. "But the timing is wrong. Besides, I saw Alice just a couple of months ago, and she definitely wasn't pregnant…"

Everything inside Kade went still when something else came to him. It couldn't be *that*.

Could it?

"The Jane agent and I posed as a couple with fertility problems, and the doctors at the Fulbright clinic had me provide some semen," Kade explained.

"Could the doctors have used it to impregnate the mother?" Grayson asked.

"I'm not sure. Maybe," Kade conceded. "The investigation didn't go as planned. Something went wrong. Someone at the clinic drugged us, and we had to fight our way out of there. But maybe during that time we were drugged, they used the semen to make her pregnant."

The doctor shook his head. "If the birth mother was an agent, then why wasn't her DNA in the system?"

It was Grayson who answered. "If she was in deep-cover ops, a Jane, they don't enter those agents' DNA into the normal law enforcement databases. The Bureau doesn't want anyone to know they work for the FBI."

His brother was right. The odds were slim to none that Special Agent Bree Winston's DNA would be in any database other than the classified one at FBI Headquarters in Quantico, Virginia.

Kade forced his eyes open, and his gaze immediately landed on the baby that Grayson was holding. The newborn was awake now, and she had turned her head in his direction. She was looking at him.

Kade swallowed hard.

He felt the punch, and it nearly robbed him of his breath. The doctor was right. He should have sat down for this.

The love was there. Instant and strong. Deep in his heart and his gut, he knew the test had been right.

This was his baby.

His little girl.

Even though he'd had no immediate plans for fatherhood, that all changed in an instant. He knew he loved her, would do whatever it took to be a good father to her. But he also knew she'd been abandoned. That left Kade with one big question.

Where was her mother?

Where was Bree?

And by God, if something had gone on at the clinic, why hadn't she told him? Why had she kept something like this a secret?

Kade pulled in his breath, hoping it would clear his head. It didn't, but he couldn't take the time to adjust to the bombshell that had just slammed right into him.

He leaned down and brushed a kiss on his baby girl's cheek. She blinked, and she stared at him as if trying to figure out who the heck he was.

"Take care of her for me," Kade said to his brother. "I'll be back as soon as I can."

Grayson nodded and stared at him, too. "You know where the mother is?"

He shook his head. Kade had no idea, since he hadn't heard anything from her since that assignment eight and a half months ago at the Fulbright clinic. Right now, he was sure of only one thing. If the baby was here and Bree wasn't, that meant she was either dead or in big trouble.

Kade had to find Bree *fast*.

Chapter Two

Bree heard the pitiful sound, a hoarse moan, and it took her a moment to realize that the sound had come from her own throat.

She opened her eyes and looked around for anything familiar. Anything that felt right.

Nothing did.

She was in some kind of room. A hotel maybe. A cheap one judging from the looks of things. The ceiling had moldy water stains, and those stains moved in and out of focus. Ditto for the dingy, paint-blistered walls. The place smelled like urine and other things she didn't want to identify.

What she did want to identify was where she was and why she was there. Bree was certain there was a good reason for it, but she couldn't remember what that reason was. It was hard to remember anything with a tornado going on inside her head.

She forced herself into a sitting position on the narrow bed. Beneath her the lumpy mattress creaked and shifted. She automatically reached for her gun and cell phone that should have been on the nightstand.

But they weren't there.

Something was wrong.

Everything inside her screamed for her to get out

right away. She had to get to a phone. She had to call…
somebody. But she couldn't remember who. Still, if
she could just get to a phone, Bree was certain she'd
remember.

She put her feet on the threadbare carpet and glanced
down at her clothes. She had on a loose dress that was
navy blue with tiny white flowers. She was wearing a
pair of black flat leather shoes.

The clothing seemed as foreign to her as the hotel
room and the absence of her gun and phone. She wasn't
a dress person, and she didn't have to remember all the
details of her life to realize that. No. She was a jeans
and shirt kind of woman unless she was on the job, and
then she wore whatever the assignment dictated.

Was she on some kind of assignment here?

She didn't have the answer to that, either. But the
odds were, yes, this was the job. Too bad she couldn't
remember exactly what this job was all about.

Bree took a deep breath and managed to stand. Not
easily. She had to slap her hand on the wall just to stay
upright, and she started for the door.

Just as the doorknob moved.

Oh, God. Someone was trying to get in the room,
and with her questionable circumstances, she doubted
this would be a friendly encounter. Not good. She could
barely stand so she certainly wasn't in any shape to
fight off anyone with her bare hands. Still, she might
not have a choice.

"Think," she mumbled to herself. What undercover
role was she playing here? What was she supposed to
say or do to the person trying to get in? She might need
those answers to stay alive.

"Bree?" someone called out. It was followed by a
heavy knock on the rickety door.

She didn't answer. Couldn't. The dizziness hit her hard again, and she had no choice but to sink back down onto the bed. *Great.* At this rate, she'd be dead in a minute. Maybe less.

"Bree?" the person called out again. It was a man, and his voice sounded a little familiar. "It's me, Kade Ryland. Open up."

Kade Ryland? The dizzy spell made it almost impossible to think, but his name, like his voice, was familiar. Too bad she couldn't piece that hint of familiarity with some facts. Especially one fact...

Could she trust him?

"Don't trust anyone," she heard herself mumble, and that was the most familiar thing she'd experienced since she'd first awakened in this god-awful room.

She braced herself for the man to knock again or call out her name. But there was a sharp bashing sound, and the door flew open as he kicked it in.

Bree tried to scramble away from him while she fumbled to take off her shoe and use it as a weapon. She didn't succeed at either.

The man who'd called himself Kade Ryland came bursting into the room, along with a blast of hot, humid air from the outside.

The first thing she saw was his gun, a Glock. Since there was no way she could dodge a bullet in the tiny space or run into the adjoining bathroom, Bree just sat there and waited for him to come closer. That way, she could try to grab his gun if it became necessary.

However, he didn't shoot.

And he didn't come closer.

He just stood there and took in the room with a sweeping glance. A cop's glance that she recognized because it's what she would have done. And then he turned that intense cop's look on her.

Bree fought the dizziness so she could study his face, his expression. He was in his early thirties. Dark brown hair peeking out from a Stetson that was the same color, gray eyes, about six-two and a hundred and eighty pounds. He didn't exactly look FBI with his slightly too-long hair, day-old stubble, well-worn jeans, black T-shirt and leather jacket, but she had some vague memory that he was an agent like her.

Was that memory right?

Or was he the big bad threat that her body seemed to think he was?

"Bree?" he repeated. His gaze locked with hers, and as he eased closer, his cowboy boots thudded on the floor. "What happened to you?"

She failed at her first attempt to speak and had to clear her throat. "I, uh, was hoping you could tell me." Mercy, she sounded drunk. "I'm having trouble remembering how I got here. Or why." She glanced around the seedy room again. "Where is *here* exactly?"

He cursed. It was ripe and filled with concern. She was right there on the same page with him—but that didn't mean she trusted him.

"You're in a motel in one of the worst parts of San Antonio," he told her. "It isn't safe for you to be here."

She hadn't thought for a minute that it was. Everything about it, including this man, put her on full alert.

But how had she gotten to this place?

"I was at my apartment," she mumbled. Was that right? She thought about it a second. Yes. That part was right. "But I don't know how I got from there to here."

Kade shut the door, though it was no longer connected to the top hinge, and he slipped his gun back into the leather shoulder holster beneath his jacket.

"Come on," he said, catching onto her arm. He gave a heavy sigh. "I need to get you to a doctor."

"No!" Bree couldn't say it fast enough. She didn't want to add another person—another stranger—to this mix. She shook off his grip. "I just need a phone. I have to call someone right away."

"Yeah. You need to call your boss, Special Agent Randy Cooper. Or Coop as you call him. But I can do that for you while you're seeing the doctor."

Coop. That name was familiar, too, and it seemed right that he was her boss. It also seemed right that she'd get answers from him. Especially since this cowboy agent didn't seem to be jumping to provide her with the vital information that she needed. She had to know if she could trust him or if she should try to escape.

Bree stared up at him. "Am I on assignment?"

Kade stared at her, too. Stared as if she'd lost her mind. He leaned down, closer, so they were eye to eye. "What the heck happened to you?"

She opened her mouth and realized she didn't have an answer. "I don't know. How did I get here?" She tried to get up again. "I need to call Coop. He'll know. He'll tell me why I'm here."

"Coop doesn't have a clue what happened to you."

That got her attention and not in a good way. "What do you mean?"

Kade moved even closer. "Bree, you've been missing nearly a year."

Oh, mercy. That info somehow got through the dizziness, but it didn't make sense. Nothing about this did. What the heck was wrong with her?

Bree shook her head. "Impossible."

He shoved up the sleeve of his black leather jacket and showed her a watch. He tapped his index finger on the date. June 13.

"June 13?" she repeated. Obviously, he thought that would mean something to her. It didn't. That was because Bree had no idea what the date should be. Nor did she know the date of that last clear memory—when she'd been at her apartment.

"I didn't know you were missing at first, not until a little over a month ago," he continued. His voice trailed off to barely a whisper, but then he cleared his throat.

"What's the last thing you remember before this place?" Kade asked. But he didn't just ask. He demanded it. He seemed to be angry about something, and judging from his stare turned glare, she was at least the partial source of that anger.

But what had she done to rile him?

She cursed that question because she didn't have an answer for it or any of the others.

Bree pushed her hair from her face. That's when she noticed her hands were trembling. Her mouth was bone dry, too. "Someone drugged me, didn't they?"

"Probably. Your pupils are dilated, and there's not a drop of color in your face," he let her know. "What's the last thing you remember?" he repeated.

She forced herself to think. "I remember you. We were on assignment together at the Fulbright Clinic. Someone figured out I was an agent, and they drugged us. We had to shoot our way out of there."

Bree glanced down at the thin scar on her left arm where a bullet had grazed her. It wasn't red and raw as it should be. It was well-healed. But that couldn't be right.

"And?" Kade prompted.

Bree shook her head. There was no *and*. "How long ago was that?"

"Nine and a half months." His jaw muscles turned to iron. She might have been dizzy, but she didn't miss the nine month reference. *Nine months.* As in just the right amount of time to have had a baby.

Her gaze flew back to him. This time Bree took a much longer and harder look at the cowboy. His face was more than just familiar. Those features. That body. Kade Ryland was drop-dead hot, and yes, she could imagine herself sleeping with him.

But had she?

She wasn't a person who engaged in casual sex or sex with a fellow agent.

"We didn't have sex, did we?" she asked.

Something shot through his ice-gray eyes. Some emotion she didn't understand. "No," he concluded. "But there was an opportunity for you to get pregnant. We were in a fertility clinic, after all."

Oh, mercy. Had the doctors in the clinic done something to her? No, Bree decided. She would have known. She would have remembered that.

Wouldn't she?

"After the shoot-out, other agents moved in to arrest the two security guards who tried to kill us," Kade continued. "But we didn't manage to apprehend everyone involved. Key evidence was missing, but the FBI decided to send in other agents to do the investigation since my identity had been compromised."

Yes. That sounded right. It wasn't an actual memory, though. None of this was, and that nearly sent Bree into a panic.

"And then you called your boss," Kade continued,

his voice calm despite the thick uneasiness in the room. "You said you were taking some vacation time."

Still no memory. Bree just sat there, listening, and praying he would say something to clear the cobwebs in her head and that it would all come back to her.

"Two weeks later when you were supposed to check back in with Coop, you didn't. You disappeared." Kade caught her chin, forced it up. "Bree, I need you to think. Where have you been all these months?"

Again, she tried to think, to remember. She really tried. But nothing came. She saw flashes of herself in Kade's arms. He was naked. And with his hard muscled body pressed against hers. He'd kissed her as if they were engaged in some kind of battle—fierce, hot, relentless.

Despite the dizziness, she felt her body go warm.

Bad timing, Bree, she reminded herself.

"You, uh, have some kind of tattoo on your back? It's like a coin or something?" She phrased it as a question just in case she was getting her memories mixed up, but she doubted she could ever mix up a man like Kade with anyone else.

"A concho," he supplied. "With back to back double *R*'s, for my family's ranch. You remember that?"

A ranch. Yes, he looked like a cowboy all right. She'd bet he wasn't wearing those jeans, Stetson and boots to make a fashion statement. No, he was a cowboy to the core, and that FBI badge and standard issue Glock didn't diminish that one bit.

"We kissed," she recalled. Now, *here* was a crystal clear memory. His mouth on hers. A fake kiss with real fire. And a cowboy with an unforgettable taste. "To create the cover of a happily married couple."

"But we didn't have sex," he clarified.

No. They hadn't, and she was reasonably sure she would have remembered sleeping with Kade. She glanced at him again and took out the *reasonably* part.

She would have remembered *that.*

"How did you find me?" Bree asked. There were so many questions and that seemed a good place to start.

"I set up a missing person's hotline and plastered your picture all over the state. I didn't say anything about you working for the FBI," he added, just as she was on the verge of protesting.

The last part of his explanation caused her to breathe just a little easier. As a deep-cover agent, the last thing she wanted was her picture out there. Still, his plan had worked because here he was. He'd found her.

But why had he been looking?

Was he working for her boss, Coop?

"An hour ago, I got a tip from an anonymous caller using a prepaid cell," Kade continued. "The person disguised their voice but said I'd find you here at the Tree-top Motel, room 114. The person also said you were sick and might need a doctor."

An anonymous caller using a prepaid cell. That set off alarms in her head. "Someone drugged me and dumped me here. That same someone might have been your caller."

"That's my guess." He paused, huffed and rubbed his hand over his forehead as if he had a raging headache. "Look, there's no easy way to say this, so I'm just going to put it out there so you can start dealing with it. I think someone in the fertility clinic inseminated you with the semen they got from me...."

Kade hesitated, maybe to let that sink in. But how the heck could that sink in?

Bree gasped and looked down at her stomach. "I'm

not pregnant. If I were, I'd be about ready to deliver." She stretched the dress across her stomach to show him there was no baby bulge.

"You've already delivered, Bree. A baby girl. She's about seven weeks old."

She heard that sound. A hoarse moan that tore its way from her own throat. "You're lying." He *had* to be lying.

Kade didn't take back what he'd said. He just stood there, waiting.

Bree tried to figure out how she could disprove the lie, and she glanced down at her stomach again.

"Go ahead," Kade prompted. "Look at your belly. I don't know if you'll have stretch marks or not, but there'll likely be some kind of changes."

Bree frantically shook her head, but her adamant denial didn't stop her from standing. Still wobbling, she turned away from Kade and shoved up the loose dress. She was wearing white bikini panties that she didn't recognize, but the unfamiliar underwear was only the tip of the proverbial iceberg.

Just slightly above the top of her panties was a scar.

Unlike the one on her arm, this one still had a pink tinge to it. It had healed, but the incision had happened more recently than the gunshot injury.

Probably about seven weeks ago.

Bree let go of the dress so it would drop back down. "What did you do to me?" She turned back to him. She would have pounded her fists against his chest if he hadn't caught her hands. "What did you do?"

"Nothing. It wasn't me. It was someone in the Fulbright Clinic." Now it was Kade's turn to groan, and that was her first clue that he was as stunned by this as she was.

They stood there, gazes locked. Her heart was beating so hard that she thought it might come out of her chest.

"Who did the C-section?" she demanded.

Kade shook his head, cursed. "I don't know. Until now, I didn't even know you'd had one, though the doctor in Silver Creek guessed. He said Leah's head was perfectly shaped, probably because she'd been delivered via C-section."

What little breath Bree had vanished. *"Leah?"*

"That's what I've been calling her. It was my grandmother's name."

"Leah," she mumbled. Oh, mercy. None of this was making sense. "What makes you think she's our child?"

"DNA tests," he said without hesitation. "I got your DNA from the classified database in Quantico and compared it to Leah's. It's a match."

There was so much coming at her that Bree could no longer breathe. Was this all true? Or maybe Kade and this baby story were figments of her drug-induced imagination. One thing was for certain. She needed to contact her boss. Coop was the only one she could trust right now.

And Coop had better tell her this was all some kind of misunderstanding.

"I need to use your cell phone," she insisted.

"You can use it in the truck." He took her by the arm. "Something bad obviously happened to you, and we need to find out what. That starts with a visit to the doctor so you have a tox screen."

Bree didn't dispute the fact that she might indeed need medical attention, but she had no reason to blindly trust Kade Ryland.

"I want to make that call now," she demanded.

Kade stared at her, huffed again and reached in his coat pocket. But reaching for his phone was as far as he got. There was a noise just outside the door, and despite the drug haze, it was a sound that Bree immediately recognized.

Footsteps.

Kade drew his gun, and in the same motion, he shoved her behind him.

But it was too late.

Bree heard a swishing sound. One that she also recognized. Someone had a gun rigged with a silencer.

And a bullet came tearing through the thin wooden door.

Chapter Three

Kade threw his weight against Bree to push her out of the line of fire. She landed hard against the wall, and Kade had no choice but to land hard against her.

Another bullet came through the door, splintering out a huge chunk of the already-rickety wood. No one called out for them to surrender. No one bashed in the room to hold them at gunpoint.

And that meant the gunman had one goal: to kill Bree and him.

Later, he would kick himself for coming here without backup, but he'd been in such a hurry to rescue Bree that Kade had put standard procedures aside so he could get to her before she left the motel. Or before she was killed or kidnapped again. Finding her had been critical. But now the challenge was to get her out of there alive.

It was a risk, anything was at this point, but Kade moved from the wall so he could kick the dresser against the door. He gave it another shove to anchor it in place.

"That won't stop him for long," Bree mumbled.

No. It wouldn't. But if the gunman had wanted to get inside, he could have easily knocked down the door before he started shooting. Firing through the door had likely been his way of trying to strike first without risking a direct showdown. If so, he knew Kade was armed. Maybe he even knew that Kade was an agent.

But who was he?

And why attack them?

Kade wanted those answers, and maybe he could get them from this Bozo if he could keep the guy alive. Of course, rescuing Bree was his first priority.

Kade had to do something to keep some space between the danger and Bree, so he fired directly into the door. Unlike the gunman's shots, the one he fired was a loud thick blast that echoed through the room. He didn't wait to see if he'd hit the target. He had to get Bree out of there.

Unfortunately, their options sucked.

Kade shoved her into the bathroom, such as it was. Barely five feet across with only a toilet and what was once a shower stall.

The tile was cracked and filthy, but the room had one redeeming feature: a window that faced the back side of the motel. He knew it was there because he'd done a snapshot surveillance of the place before he ever knocked on Bree's door. The gunman would have to run around the entire length of the building to get to that window. Well, unless he had a partner with him. Kade hoped that wasn't the case. One gunman was more than enough.

Another shot came into the bedroom.

Kade returned fire, this time a double tap that would hopefully send a message—he would kill to get Bree out of there. He darn sure hadn't come this far to lose her before he got the answers to his questions.

Bree was still more than a little unsteady on her feet so Kade shoved her deeper in the bathroom, kicked the door shut and locked it. The lock was as rickety as the rest of the place, and it wouldn't give them much protection if the gunman came blasting in, but it might buy them a few critical seconds, just enough time to get out.

He hurried to the window. It popped right open, and he looked out in the thin alley that separated the motel from an equally seedy-looking bar. Both ends of the alley were open, and there were no signs of a backup gunman, but it would still be a long dangerous run to his truck.

"I'll go first to make sure it's safe," he told Bree. "You follow me. Got that?"

She gave him a look, and for a moment he thought Bree might refuse. For a good reason, too. She didn't trust him.

And why should she?

Bree was no doubt trying to absorb everything he'd just dumped on her, and Kade knew from personal experience that coming to terms with unexpected parenthood wasn't something that could happen in five minutes—especially after the trauma Bree had been through. And the trauma wasn't over.

"You have no choice," Kade told her. He moved his truck keys from his jeans pocket to his jacket so they'd be easier to reach. "If we stay here, we both die."

She shook her head as if trying to clear it, or argue with him, but still didn't move. Not until another bullet bashed through the room.

And more.

Someone was moving the dresser that Kade had used to block the door. That *someone* was now in the motel room just a few yards away with only a paper-thin wall and equally thin bathroom door between them.

Bree's eyes widened. She obviously understood what was happening now. She caught his arm and shoved

him against the window. Kade grabbed the sill, hoist-
ing himself up and slithered through the narrow open-
ing. He landed on his feet with his gun ready, and he
looked up.

No Bree.

For one heart-stopping moment Kade thought she
might have decided to take her chances with the gunman, but then he saw her hand on the sill. She was
struggling to keep a grip. And Kade cursed himself
again. The drugs had made her too weak to lever herself up.

While he tried to keep watch on both sides of the
alley, Kade latched onto her wrist and pulled hard. She
finally tumbled forward and landed with a jolt right in
his arms. He didn't have time to make sure she was okay
or even carry her since he had to keep his shooting hand
free. Kade put her on her feet, grabbed her by the shoulder and started running in the direction of his truck.

They were already on borrowed time. By Kade's
calculations, it'd been twenty seconds or longer since
the gunman had fired. That meant he could have already made it into the bathroom and have seen that
they weren't there. He could try to kill them by shooting through the window, or else he could be heading
around the building straight toward them.

"I should have a gun," Bree mumbled.

Yeah, she should. That would be a big help right
about now because Kade knew for a fact she could
shoot. However, since he couldn't take the time to pull
his backup weapon from his ankle holster, he ran as
fast as he could with a groggy, dazed woman in tow.

Finally, he spotted his dark blue truck.

But Kade also heard something.

He glanced behind them and saw someone he didn't

want to see. A guy wearing camo pants and jacket came around the far end of the building. He was also armed, and he pointed a handgun directly at Kade and Bree.

There wasn't time to get to his truck. No time to do much of anything except get out of the line of fire. So Kade shoved Bree to the ground, right against the exterior wall of the hotel, and he followed on top of her. Not a second too soon. The guy pulled the trigger.

The shot slammed into the wall.

Kade turned, took aim and returned fire.

Their attacker dived to the side but not far enough. Kade could still see him, and he wanted the SOB temporarily out of the picture so he could get Bree safely out of there. Of course, he might have to settle for killing the guy. That would mean no answers, but it was better than the alternative.

Kade sent another shot his way.

And another.

He cursed when the guy moved, causing the bullets to strafe into the ground. But the third was a charm because the gunman finally scrambled back behind the building.

Bree was trembling and as white as paper when Kade came off the ground and yanked her to her feet. She had been under fire before, but probably not while defenseless. Kade kept watch behind them, but he got them running toward the truck again. He also did some praying that a second gunman wasn't near his vehicle.

Kade fired another shot in the direction of the gunman. Maybe it would keep him pinned down long enough for them to escape.

Maybe.

He let go of Bree so he could take out his keys, and he pressed the button to unlock the doors. Thankfully,

Bree ran without his help, and they made a beeline for the truck.

Kade saw the gunman again, but he didn't stop to fire. Instead, he threw open the truck door. Bree did the same on the passenger's side, and they both dived in.

"Watch out!" Bree shouted. "He's coming after us."

"I see him," Kade let her know.

He lowered the window, just enough to allow himself room to fire another shot. Just enough to keep the gunman at bay for a few more seconds.

Kade started the engine and slammed his foot on the accelerator. He didn't exactly make a silent exit out of the parking lot. The tires howled against the asphalt, but Kade figured anyone within a quarter mile had already heard the gunfight and either reported it or run away.

In this neighborhood, he was betting it was the latter.

"Keep watch," he told Bree.

While he took out his phone, he glanced around to make sure they weren't being followed. Then, he glanced at Bree.

Man, she was still way too pale, and she was sucking in air so fast she might hyperventilate. In the four days he had spent with her undercover, he'd never seen her like this, and Kade hoped she could hold herself together for just a little while longer until he could get her out of there and to a doctor.

Since he didn't want to spend a lot of time making all the calls he needed, Kade made the one that he knew would get the ball rolling. He pressed in the number for his brother, Lt. Nate Ryland, at San Antonio police headquarters. Nate answered on the first ring because he was no doubt waiting for news about Bree.

"I found her at the Treetop Motel," Kade said. That alone would be a bombshell since over the past month they'd had nine false reports of Bree's location. "But there was a gunman. Caucasian. Brown hair. About six-two. One-seventy. No distinguishing marks."

Nate cursed and mumbled something about Kade being a stubborn ass for not waiting for backup. "I'll get a team out there right away," Nate assured him, and it was the exact assurance Kade needed. "What about you? Where are you taking her?"

"The hospital. Not here in San Antonio. I'm driving her to Silver Creek." Kade didn't say that too loud, though Bree no doubt heard it, anyway. "Call me if you find anything at the hotel. I'll let you know when I have answers."

"I don't want to go to a hospital," Bree said the moment he ended the call. She was trembling, but she had her attention fastened to the side mirror, no doubt checking to see if they were being followed. "I just want to find out what happened to me."

So did Kade. But first he had to make sure the gunman wasn't on their tail. Then the hospital whether she wanted to go there or not.

While Bree was being checked out by a doctor, he could start the calls and the paperwork. It wouldn't be pretty. He would have to explain to his boss and his brothers why he hadn't waited for backup after receiving that anonymous tip about Bree's location. It probably wasn't going to fly if he told them that he had a gut feeling that she was in danger.

And he'd been right.

Still, gut instincts didn't look good on paper, and he would get his butt chewed out because of it. Kade figured it would be worth it. After all, he'd gotten Bree out of harm's way.

Well, for now.

"He's not following us," Bree concluded. She swallowed hard and looked at him.

Kade looked at her too out of the corner of his eye. She had certainly been through an ordeal. Her dark brown hair had been choppily cut and was mussed well beyond the point of making a fashion statement. And then there was the dress. It hung on her like a sack. There were dark circles under her drug-dazed eyes. Her lips were chapped raw. Still, she managed to look darn attractive.

And yeah, he was stupid enough to notice.

It was also easy to notice that Bree had passed on those cat-green eyes to their daughter.

She opened her mouth, and for a moment Kade thought she might ask about Leah. But she didn't. She snatched his phone from his hand.

"I'm calling my supervisor," Bree insisted.

Kade didn't stop her, though he knew Randy Cooper didn't have the answers that Bree wanted. That's because Kade had spent a lot of time with the agent over the past month and a half.

She must have remembered the number because she pressed it in without hesitation and put the call on speaker. "Coop," she said when the man answered.

"Bree," he said just as quickly. "Are you all right?"

"No." With that single word, her breath broke, and tears sprang to her eyes. She tried to blink them back, but more just came.

"The last lead paid off," Kade informed Coop. "She was at the Treetop Motel here in San Antonio, but so was a gunman. The informant could have set us up to be killed."

Coop cursed. "Either of you hurt?"

"I'm fine," Kade assured him. "Not so sure about Bree—"

"Where have I been all these months?" she interrupted.

"I don't know," Coop answered. He gave a weary sigh. "But trust me, we'll find out."

Yeah. They would. Step one was done. Kade had located Bree, and now that he had her, he could start unraveling this crazy puzzle that had resulted in the birth of their daughter.

"I need to see you ASAP," Coop told her. "How soon can you get her here, Kade?"

"Not soon," Kade let him know. "Someone drugged her, and even though it looks as if it's wearing off, she needs to see a doctor."

"I can arrange that," Coop insisted.

Of course Coop could, but if Kade took Bree to FBI headquarters, she'd be sucked into the system. Exams, interviews, paperwork. That had to wait because the FBI wouldn't put Leah first.

Kade would.

He had to find out if the gunman meant Leah was now in danger, too. Kade had a hard time just stomaching that thought, but it wouldn't do him any good to bury his head in the sand.

"Is it true, Coop?" Bree asked. "Did I really have a baby?"

Coop took some time answering. "Yes," was all he said.

Bree groaned, squeezed her eyes shut and the phone dropped into her lap. She buried her face in her hands. She wasn't hyperventilating yet, but she was about to fall apart.

"Coop, we'll call you back. In the meantime, my

brother Lt. Nate Ryland is on his way to the hotel crime scene and is trying to track down this gunman. We need to find this guy," Kade emphasized, though Coop already knew that.

Because the gunman could be the key to unraveling this. Well, unless he was just a hired gun. But even then, that was a start since they could find out who'd paid him to kill them.

Coop began to argue with Kade's refusal of his order to bring Bree in, but Kade took the phone from her lap and ended the call. He also made another turn so he could check to make sure they weren't being followed. Things looked good in that department but not with Bree. She kept her hands over her face. Clamped her teeth over her bottom lip. And then she made that sound. Half groan, half sob.

Hell. That did it.

Kade hooked his arm around her and dragged her across the seat toward him. Much to his surprise, she didn't fight him. She dropped her head on his shoulder.

For a moment, anyway.

Just a moment.

Her head whipped up, and she met his gaze. She blinked. Shook her head and got a strange look in her eyes.

"I have to keep watch," she insisted. Bree moved back across the seat and glanced at the mirror. Her breathing got faster again. "There's a black sedan behind us."

"Yeah." Kade was fully aware of that. "But I don't think it's following us. It just exited onto this road." To prove his point, he made another turn, and the car didn't follow.

That didn't settle Bree's breathing much. She started

to chew on her bottom lip. "You told Coop that your brother was helping us. He's a cop?"

Kade nodded. "San Antonio PD. All four of my brothers are in law enforcement. We've been working to find you ever since someone abandoned Leah at the hospital."

"Leah," Bree repeated, and she slid her hand over her stomach. "We didn't have sex," she tossed out there.

"No. But someone in the fertility clinic obviously inseminated you."

"Hector McClendon," Bree said, and it wasn't exactly a question.

Kade suspected the man, as well. Hector McClendon had been head of the Fulbright Fertility Clinic and was the main target of their undercover investigation that had started all of this.

"McClendon said he wasn't aware of the illegal activity going on at his own clinic," Kade reminded her.

"Right," she mumbled, sarcasm dripping from her voice. "Stored embryos were being sold without the owners' permission or knowledge. Illegal immigrants were being used as surrogates and kept in deplorable conditions. Babies were being auctioned to the highest bidder. We were pretty sure McClendon knew what was going on." Bree looked at Kade. "Please tell me he's behind bars."

Kade hated to be the bearer of more bad news. "No. None of the evidence we got from the clinic implicated McClendon in any of the serious crimes."

And it hadn't been for Kade or the FBI's lack of trying.

"But McClendon ordered those two security guards to kill us," Bree pointed out.

"No proof of that, either. The guards are in custody,

but they're insisting they acted alone, because they thought we were a threat to the other patients. They claim they had no idea we were agents."

"Right," she repeated.

Kade had to agree with that, too. But the guards weren't spilling anything, probably because they knew it would be impossible to prove their intent to murder without corroboration from someone else. So far, that hadn't happened, and Kade suspected the guards would ultimately accept a plea deal for much lesser charges.

"The only two people arrested so far have been McClendon's son, Anthony, who was a doctor at the clinic and a nurse named Jamie Greer," he explained. "They're both out on bond, awaiting trial."

Bree repeated the names. "Just because there's no evidence, it doesn't mean McClendon's innocent of kidnapping and doing God knows what to me."

Kade tried to keep his voice calm. "True, but if he did it, he's not confessing. Still, he has the money and the resources to have held you all this time."

She shook her head. "But why?"

Now it was Kade's turn to shake his head. "I don't know. There were no ransom demands for you. Leah wasn't hurt. In fact, she was dropped off at the hospital probably less than a day after she was born."

She shuddered, maybe at the thought of her kidnapping. Maybe at the way Leah had been abandoned.

"And if McClendon had wanted me dead," Bree finished, "then why not kill me after the C-section? Heck, why not just kill me after taking me from my apartment?"

This is where Kade's theory came to an end. "I was hoping you'd have those answers."

Bree groaned. "I don't! I don't remember any of that."

He reached over and touched her arm. Rubbed lightly. Hoping it would soothe her. "But you can with help. That's why I'm taking you to the hospital."

She opened her mouth, probably to repeat that she didn't want to go, but she stopped. And gasped. "What if the gunman goes after the baby?"

"He won't." Kade hoped. "She's at my family's ranch with my brother. He's a deputy sheriff and can protect her."

Bree frantically shook her head and pushed his hand away so she could latch onto his arm. "Hurry. You have to get to her now."

There's no way Kade could stay calm after that. "Why?"

"Hurry," Bree repeated. Tears spilled down her cheeks. "Because I remember. Oh, God. I remember."

Chapter Four

The memories flooded back into Bree's mind. They came so fast, so hard, that she had trouble latching onto all of them. But the one memory that was first and foremost was the danger to the baby.

Her baby.

Even though that didn't seem real, Bree had no more doubts about the child. She had indeed given birth, and at the moment that was the clearest memory she had.

"You have to get to the baby," Bree insisted.

"I'm headed there now," Kade assured her. His voice sounded more frantic than hers. "What's wrong?" he demanded. "What do you remember?"

"Pretty much everything." And Bree tested that by starting with the first thing she could recall. "The night after the botched assignment at Fulbright Fertility Clinic, I was kidnapped by a person wearing a mask."

"How did that happen?" Kade wanted to know. "And what does it have to do with Leah?"

"It has everything to do with Leah." Because it was the start of her becoming pregnant. "I came out of my apartment that night, and the person was waiting for me just outside the door. He popped me on the neck with a stun gun. I went down like a rock before I could even fight back. Then, the guy used chloroform." Yes, definitely. She recalled the sickly sweet smell of the drug.

"Chloroform," he repeated, but there was impatience in his voice now. Concern, too. "Did you get a good look at the person before you lost consciousness?"

"No." In fact, not a look at all, good or otherwise. The guy never took off his mask. "When I finally came to, I was at a house in the middle of nowhere, and the guy wasn't alone. A masked woman was with him." Bree had to pause and regroup. "You were right—they inseminated me with your baby."

He had a death grip on the steering wheel and was flying through traffic. "Why did they do that, and why do we have to hurry to get to Leah?"

Oh, this was crystal clear. Well, part of it, anyway. "More than once they said that the baby was to get me and you to *cooperate*."

"Cooperate?" he questioned. "With what?"

"I don't know. And it's not that I don't remember. They didn't say how they would use the child. But I'm figuring they'll go after her, especially now that they no longer have me."

Kade cursed, snatched up his phone and made a call. Hopefully to one of those brothers he'd mentioned that were in law enforcement.

"Lock down the ranch," Kade instructed to whomever was on the other end of the line. "There could be trouble. I'll be there in about twenty minutes."

He jabbed the end call button so hard that she was surprised the phone didn't break. "Who held you captive, and if they planned to use Leah to get to you and me, then why abandon her at the hospital?"

That part wasn't so crystal clear, but Bree had a theory about it. "Something must have gone wrong. Not at the beginning, but later."

Much later.

The memories came again. Like bullets, slamming into her. "I woke up after the delivery and heard my kidnappers talking," she continued. "The man told the woman he didn't get the money they'd been promised. He was furious. He was going to kill me right then and there." A shiver went through her. "Maybe the baby, too."

Kade's jaw muscles turned to iron. "What stopped them?"

Bree had to take a moment because she was reliving that horrible fear as if it were happening all over again. "The woman talked the man out of it. She said she'd take care of the baby." Bree had to choke back the emotions she'd felt then. And now. "I thought that meant…"

She couldn't finish, but she'd thought she would never see her baby alive.

"This woman must have been the one who dropped Leah off at the hospital," Kade said through clenched teeth. He turned off the interstate at the Silver Creek exit. "Leah wasn't harmed."

Relief flooded through Bree. But it didn't last long. "If the man who kidnapped me knows that she's alive…" She couldn't finish that, either.

"No one will get onto the ranch without my brothers being alerted," he promised. He didn't say anything else for several moments. "How did you escape?"

"The woman helped me again. She had on a prosthetic mask, one of those latex things that makes it impossible to see any of her real features. And she used a voice scrambler so I never heard her speak normally.

But a few hours after she disappeared with the baby, she came back and got me."

Now, here's where her memory failed. No more bullets. Only bits and pieces of images and conversations that Bree wasn't sure she could trust. Were they real or part of the nightmare she'd had all these months?

"She drugged me then and I don't know how many times after. A lot," Bree settled on saying. "The woman moved me, too. Usually to and from hotels, but a time or two, she took me to a house. I think she was trying to save me."

"Sure. And she might have made that call to let me know you were at the motel," he suggested. "The person who contacted me used a voice scrambler, too."

If so, then Bree owed that woman her life many times over. Not just for saving her, but for delivering Leah to Kade.

Except the woman had also been one of Bree's kidnappers.

If she hadn't helped keep Bree captive, then maybe none of this would have happened. And since Kade and she had come darn close to dying today, Bree wasn't ready to give the woman a free pass just yet.

"This has to go back to the Fulbright clinic," Kade said. "Hector McClendon could have masterminded all of it. His son, Anthony, and that clinic nurse, Jamie Greer, could have helped with the kidnapping. And with the delivery since Anthony is a doctor."

She couldn't argue with that. Plus, she'd seen what they really were at the clinic—criminals—and believed them capable of murder. After all, someone had tried hard to cover up everything that had gone on there.

"You said Anthony and Jamie were out on bond awaiting trial?" Bree asked.

"Yeah. And their lawyers have been stonewalling the investigation and the trials."

Great. So, not only were they suspects, both had the means and opportunity to have done this to her. In fact, they could be working as a team.

"Maybe they were looking for another way to get some leverage over us," Kade went on, "since we're the only two people who could or would testify against them. That could be why the kidnappers said they would use the baby for leverage."

True, and McClendon could have done the same, as well. Of course, if she remembered correctly, there wasn't any hard evidence against him except for some minor charges that wouldn't warrant much jail time, if any at all.

Not so far, anyway.

Nor could Kade and she testify that they'd seen him do anything illegal because they hadn't. McClendon had stayed away from the dirt, and even though Bree had tried, she hadn't been able to make a direct connection between him and the crimes.

Still, McClendon could have feared that some evidence would surface that would support their testimony. After all, Kade and she had failed to find the missing disks to the clinic's surveillance systems. Those systems were dated and still did hardcopy backups. If they'd found those, then McClendon might be in jail right now, and he couldn't have kidnapped her.

If he had been the one to honcho the kidnapping.

The agent in her reminded her to look at all the angles. To examine the evidence and situation with an unbiased eye. But it was hard to do that when someone had made Kade and her involuntary parents, and might now be placing their daughter in danger.

"You heard your male kidnapper speak," Kade continued. He took a turn off the main highway and turned onto Ryland Ranch Road. "Was it Anthony or McClendon?"

Bree had to shake her head. "Maybe. The man also used a voice scrambler whenever he was around me." Which wasn't very often. He always kept his distance from her and only came into the room after she'd been given a heavy dose of drugs. "But if I could hear interviews with Jamie and Anthony, I might be able to pick up on speech patterns."

Kade didn't respond except to pull in a long hard breath. And Bree soon realized why. He stopped directly in front of the sprawling three-story house that was surrounded by acres and acres of pasture and outbuildings.

It looked serene. Inviting. Like pictures of ranches that she'd seen in glossy Western magazines. There definitely wasn't any sign of kidnappers, gunmen or danger, but Bree still felt panic crawl through her.

The baby was inside.

Oh, mercy. She wasn't ready for this. Maybe she'd never be ready. But she especially wasn't ready with her mind in this foggy haze.

"I need a minute," she managed to say. A minute to get her breath and heartbeat tamped down. Her composure was unraveling fast. "For the record, I'd never planned on having children."

When Kade didn't say anything, Bree looked at him. She didn't exactly see empathy there. Well, not at first. But then he gave a heavy sigh and slipped his arm around her. As he'd done before, he pulled her across the seat until she was cradled against him. It felt better than it should.

Far better.

Bree knew she should be backing away. She should be trying to stay objective and focused on what had happened. Besides, she'd learned the hard way that taking this kind of comfort from a man, any man, could be a bad mistake. Especially since she could feel this steamy attraction for Kade simmering inside her. It'd been there from the first moment she'd laid eyes on him.

And it was still there now.

Getting worse, too. The comforting shoulder was getting all mixed up with the confusion, the attraction and the fact that he'd just saved her life.

Bree took another deep breath and gathered her composure. "Let's do this," she said, pushing herself away from him.

Kade lifted his eyebrow but didn't question her. Not verbally, anyway. He got out of the truck and started toward the porch. Bree followed him, and with each step she tried to steady her nerves.

She finally gave up.

Nothing could help in that department.

But then, Kade reached out and took her hand.

It was such a simple gesture. And much to her surprise and concern, she felt herself calm down. It lasted just a few seconds until Kade threw open the front door, and Bree spotted the armed dark-haired man.

Kade's brother, no doubt.

But this Ryland had a hard dangerous look that had her wanting to take a step back. She didn't. However, she did pull her hand from Kade's.

"This is my brother Mason," Kade explained. He took off his Stetson, put it on a wall hook where there were two similar ones, and he glanced around the massive foyer.

Bree glanced around, too, looking for any threats,

any gunmen. Anything other than the brother that might set off alarms in her head.

Like the house's exterior, this place screamed *home*. It looked well lived in and loved with its warm weathered wood floors and paintings of horses and cattle. There were more pictures and framed family shots in the massive living room off to her left.

"Where are the others?" Kade asked when he'd finished looking around.

"Dade's in his office watching the security cameras. After you called, I had a couple of the ranch hands take Kayla, Darcy, Eve and the kids to Grayson in town. They'll stay at the sheriff's office for a while."

Since Bree didn't recognize those names, she looked at Kade.

"Dade's another brother," he clarified. "He's a deputy sheriff like Mason here. Kayla, Darcy and Eve are all my sisters-in-law." He turned his attention to Mason but didn't say anything.

Something passed between them. A look. And Mason tipped his head to the room off the left side of the foyer. Kade caught Bree's arm and led her in that direction.

For one horrifying moment she wondered if she'd been a fool to trust Kade. After all, someone had kidnapped her and done heaven knows what to her. But that horrifying moment passed and settled like a rock-hard knot in her stomach when they walked into the living room and Bree saw the petite woman with reddish graying hair.

The woman was holding a bundle in a pink blanket.

"This is Grace Borden, one of the nannies here at the ranch," Kade said. "Grace, this is Bree Winston."

Grace offered Bree a tentative smile and then walked

toward her. As she got closer, Bree saw the tiny hand as it fluttered out from the blanket. The knot in Bree's stomach got worse. It got even tighter when Grace stopped in front of her, and Bree could see the baby nestled inside all that pink.

"This is Leah Marie Ryland," Kade volunteered. He led Bree to the sofa and had her sit down, probably because she didn't look too steady on her feet. And she wasn't. "The names of both my grandmothers."

A lot of family tradition for such a tiny little thing. "You said she's healthy?"

Kade nodded. "She just had her checkup, and she's nearly eight pounds now."

Bree had no idea if that was good or bad. And the terrifying feeling returned in spades when Grace came closer and held out the baby for Bree to take. The nanny must have picked up on Bree's uneasiness because she shot Kade a questioning glance. The moment he gave another nod, Grace eased the baby into Bree's arms.

It probably wasn't a normal reaction, but Bree gasped.

She'd never held any living thing this tiny, and Leah felt too fragile for Bree to trust her hands. Her breath stalled in her throat. In fact, everything seemed to stop.

"I'll be in the kitchen if you need me," Grace whispered.

"I need you to call Dr. Mickelson," Kade told her. "If he can, have him come out to the ranch right away to give Bree a checkup. Explain that she'll need lab work done."

That made sense. Maybe they could learn what she'd been drugged with. Considering the female kidnapper had seemingly tried to keep Bree alive, maybe the drug wasn't addictive or harmful. Ditto for the drugs they'd given her when she was pregnant.

Grace verified that she would indeed call the doctor and walked out of the room. The silence came immediately. Awkward and long. Bree couldn't say anything. She could only stare at the baby's face.

"She's got my hair and coloring," Kade said. "Your green eyes, though."

Yes, those curls were indeed dark brown, and there were lots of them. Bree couldn't see the baby's eyes because she was sound asleep. But she could see the shape of her face. That was Kade's, too.

Until Bree had seen the baby, she'd been about to question the DNA test that Kade said he'd run. She had figured to ask him to repeat it, just to be sure. But a repeat wasn't necessary. Kade was right: Leah was a genetic mix of Ryland and Winston blood.

And that required a deep breath.

Because she knew this baby was indeed hers.

Oh, mercy. Not good. She had lousy DNA, and that's why she'd never intended on passing it on to a helpless little baby.

"Here," Bree managed to say, and she quickly handed Leah to Kade. Despite her wobbly legs, she got up so she could put some distance between Kade and her.

Kade cuddled the baby closer to him, brushed a kiss on her cheek. The gesture was so loving. But the glare he aimed at her wasn't. Far from it. She'd obviously riled him again, and he had no trouble showing it.

"I don't have a normal life," Bree blurted out. "I'm always deep undercover. Always living a lie."

That didn't ease his scowl.

"Besides, I'm no good with kids." Even though looking at that tiny face made her wish that she was. There was something about that face that made her want to do what Kade had done—brush a kiss on her cheek.

Kade's scowl ended only because Leah made a sound. Not a cry exactly, more like a whimper. And he began to rock her gently as if it were the most natural thing in the world.

"I was raised in foster care," she added. Heaven knows why she'd volunteered that. Maybe to stop him from scowling at her again. Yes, it was true, and it was also true that her childhood had been so nightmarish that she'd vowed never to have children of her own.

And technically she hadn't broken that vow.

But someone had overridden her decision, and Kade was holding the proof in his arms.

Kade kissed the baby again, stood and placed her in a white carrier seat that was on the coffee table just inches away. Leah stirred a little, but she didn't wake up. He put his hands on his hips and stared at Bree.

"It's all right." His jaw was tight again, and his gray eyes had turned frosty. "I don't expect anything from you."

It felt as if he'd slugged her, and it took Bree several moments to recover and gather her breath. "What the heck does that mean?"

Kade shrugged. Not easily. The muscles were obviously locked tight there, too. "It's clear you're not comfortable with this."

"And you were?" Bree fired back.

"I am now. She's my daughter, and I'll raise her." He started to turn away, but Bree caught his arm and whirled him back around to face her.

"Now, just a minute. I didn't say I wouldn't raise her. I just need time. You've had seven weeks to adjust to being a dad," she reminded him. "I've had an hour, and for a good part of that time we've been ducking bullets and nearly getting killed."

The mini tirade drained her, but Bree stayed on her feet so she could face him. They weren't exactly eye to eye since she was a good seven inches shorter than he was, but she held his gaze.

And she saw the exact moment he backed down.

Kade mumbled some profanity and scrubbed his hand over his face. "I'm sorry. It's just that I love Leah, and I figured you'd feel the same."

"I do!" The words came flying out of her, and so did the heart-stopping realization that followed.

Bree looked at that tiny face again. Her daughter. The baby she'd carried for all those months while being held captive. She felt the tears burn her eyes, and Bree cursed them and tried to blink them back.

"I tried not to think of her as a real baby," Bree said, her voice barely a whisper. "Because I wasn't sure we would make it out of that place alive."

Oh, mercy. The confession brought on more blasted tears. Bree hated them because she wasn't a whiner, and she darn sure didn't want Kade to think she was trying to milk some sympathy from him.

Kade cursed again and called himself a bad name before he moved toward her. Bree wanted to tell him it wasn't a good time to offer her a shoulder to cry on. She was too weak and vulnerable. But Kade pulled her into his arms before she could protest.

And then she was glad he had.

Bree dropped her head on Kade's shoulder and let his strong arms support her. She felt that strength, and the equally strong attraction.

Good grief.

Didn't she have enough on her plate without adding

lust to the mix? Of course, maybe it was a little more than lust since Kade and she had this whole parenthood bond going on.

She pulled back, looked up at him. "This holding is nice, but it's not a good idea."

His left eyebrow cocked. "Considering what you've been through, you've earned the right to lean on somebody."

But not you.

She kept that to herself, but it was best if she kept Kade out of this emotionally charged equation. There was still so much to figure out. So many questions...

First though, she wanted to get acquainted with her daughter.

Bree eased out of Kade's grip and walked to the carrier seat that was lined with pale pink fabric and frilly lace. She touched her finger to Leah's cheek, and Bree was more than a little surprised when the baby's eyes opened.

Yes, they were green like hers.

Leah stared at her. Studying Bree, as if trying to figure out who she was.

"I'm your mother, little one," Bree whispered. "Your mom," she corrected. Less formal. Even though both felt foreign to Bree's vocabulary. "And you're the one who kicked me all those months. With all those hard kicks, I thought you'd be a lot bigger."

The corner of Leah's mouth lifted. A smile! It warmed Bree from head to toe. Yes. Now she knew what Kade meant when he said he loved this baby. How could he not? It was something so strong, so deep that if Bree had been standing, she wouldn't have managed to stay on her feet for long.

"This is potent stuff," she mumbled.

"Oh, yeah," Kade agreed. "Wait until she coos."

Bree wasn't sure she could wait. She stood, reached into the basket and brought her baby back into her arms. Bree drew in her scent. Something that stirred feelings she thought she'd never have.

Magic. Pure magic.

It hit Bree then. This was the only person she had ever truly loved. Someone she would die to protect.

Of course, that brought back on the blasted tears, but rather than curse them, Bree sank down on the sofa and gave her daughter a good looking over. She pulled back the blanket.

"Ten fingers, ten toes," Bree mumbled.

"And a strong set of lungs," Kade supplied. He sank down next to her. "You'll hear just how loud she can be when she wants her bottle at 2:00 a.m."

Bree turned to him. "Will I be here at 2:00 a.m.?"

Kade nodded, but it wasn't exactly a wholehearted one. Yes, he'd given her that hug and some much-needed empathy, but he was holding back. And Bree didn't blame him. She was holding back, too. The problem was she didn't want to be separated from Leah.

Correction: she couldn't be.

Yes, she'd just laid eyes on her for the first time, but Bree felt like something she'd thought she would never feel.

She felt like a mother.

An incompetent one but a mother nonetheless.

"You can stay while we sort things out," Kade finally said.

Again, it wasn't a resounding yes, but Bree would take it. At this point, she would take anything she could get that would allow her to stay with this precious child.

"Things," she repeated. A lot fell under that umbrella. The danger. And the custody, of course. Living arrangements, too. She probably no longer had an apartment since she'd been gone all this time and hadn't paid rent.

Heck, did she even have a job?

"Take one thing at a time," Kade said, his Texas drawl dancing off each word.

She returned the nod. "So, what's first?"

But Kade didn't get a chance to answer. That's because Bree and he turned toward the footsteps. A moment later, Mason appeared in the doorway.

One look at his face, and Bree knew something was wrong. *No.* Not again. She automatically pulled Leah closer to her.

"We got trouble," Mason announced, and he drew his gun.

Chapter Five

Trouble. Kade was positive they'd already had enough of their share of that today.

"What's wrong?" Kade asked his brother.

Mason tipped his head toward the front of the house. "About a minute ago, a strange car turned onto the ranch road, and Dade ran the plates. The vehicle is registered to none other than Hector McClendon."

Beside him, Bree gasped. Kade knew how she felt because McClendon shouldn't be here at the ranch. After all, he was their lead suspect in too many crimes to list—including Bree's own kidnapping that had led to Leah's birth.

That stirred some strong conflicting feelings in Kade.

He loved Leah so much that he couldn't imagine life without her, but someone would pay for what had happened. His baby didn't deserve the rough start she'd gotten in life.

Kade got to his feet, the questions already forming in his head. He hadn't wanted this meeting with McClendon, but maybe they could learn something from it. Right now, he'd take any answers he could get—as long as he got them while keeping Leah safe.

Bree, too, he mentally added.

Yes, she was a trained federal agent, but she was in no shape right now to face down a snake like McClendon.

"Wait here," he told Bree. "I'll deal with this."

But she stood, anyway, and eased Leah back into the carrier. "You're not letting him near the baby."

"Not a chance. I'm not letting him in the house, period. But I do want to talk to him and see why he came. He's never been out here to see me before now, and I don't like the timing."

It was past being suspicious since it'd been less than an hour and a half since Kade had rescued Bree from that motel. Was McClendon here to finish off the job that the hired gunman had failed to do?

Kade drew his gun and headed toward the front door.

Of course, Bree didn't stay put as he'd ordered. She was right behind him.

"Have Dade keep monitoring the security feed," Kade instructed Mason. This could be a ruse that someone could use to get gunmen onto the ranch, but Mason probably already knew that. "And take Leah to Grace. I want them to stay at the back of the house until McClendon is off the grounds."

Mason hesitated, glancing first at Leah in her carrier seat and then out the front window at the approaching silver Jaguar. His brother was probably trying to decide if he should stay and play backup, but Mason thankfully picked up the carrier and hurried out of the room.

Good. That was one less thing to worry about. One less *big* thing.

Kade gave Bree one last try so he could take another worrisome issue off his list. "McClendon could be dangerous, and you're still feeling the effects of that drug."

Her chin came up, and even though he didn't know

her that well, Kade recognized the attitude. Bree wouldn't back down. Something he understood since he would have reacted the same in her position. However, because she wasn't duty ready, he eased her behind him when he headed for the door.

Kade paused at the security system so he could open the door without setting off the alarms. By the time he'd done that, McClendon was already out of his car and walking up the porch steps. His driver—aka his armed goon bodyguard, no doubt—stayed by the open car door.

Even though it'd been months since Kade had seen the man, he hadn't changed much. The same salt-and-pepper hair styled to perfection. A pricey foreign suit. Pricey shoes, too. The man was all flash. Or rather all facade. McClendon appeared to be a highly successful businessman, but at the moment he was basically unemployed and living off the millions he'd inherited from parents. Old money.

The man was also old slime.

And Kade was going to have to hang on to every bit of his composure to keep from ripping McClendon's face off. If this arrogant SOB was behind Bree's kidnapping and the insemination, then he would pay for it.

Kade positioned himself in the center of the door, blocking the way so that McClendon couldn't enter. He also blocked Bree so she couldn't get any closer. She was already way too close for Kade's comfort.

"Why are you here?" Kade demanded.

McClendon ignored the question and looked past Kade. His attention went directly to Bree, who was on her tiptoes and peering over Kade's shoulder.

"I got a call about her." McClendon jabbed his index finger in Bree's direction. "I thought I was rid of you.

Guess not. But if you're back to make more accusations about me, then you'd better think twice."

Despite Kade's attempts to block her, Bree worked her way around him, stepping to his side, and she faced McClendon head-on. "Who called you?"

McClendon's face stayed tight with anger, but he shook his head. "It was an anonymous tipster. The person used some kind of machine to alter his voice so I couldn't tell who it was. I couldn't even tell if it was a *he*. Could have been anybody for all I know."

Like the call Kade had gotten about Bree. "This person told you Bree was here? Because I only found her myself a little while ago."

"No, the person didn't say she was here, only that she was with you. I figured out the ranch part all by myself since this, after all, is your family home," McClendon smugly added.

"It's a long drive out here just to talk to Bree," Kade remarked.

The man made a sound of agreement. "Let's just say the anonymous caller piqued my interest. Plus, I wanted to make sure Agent Winston here wasn't trying to pin more bogus charges on me."

Kade wished he had a charge, any charge, he could pin on the man. Maybe he could arrest him for trespassing, but that wouldn't get him behind bars.

"So, why do you look like death warmed over?" McClendon asked Bree.

"Because I've had a bad day. A bad year," she corrected in a snarl. "Someone kidnapped me. Maybe you? Or maybe someone working for you? Maybe even the Neanderthal standing by your car." Bree aimed her own finger at him, though unlike McClendon's, hers was shaky. "And that someone had me inseminated. What do you know about that, huh?"

McClendon flexed his eyebrows. Maybe from surprise, but Kade seriously doubted it. In fact, McClendon might have personal knowledge of every detail of this investigation.

"I know nothing about it," the man insisted. "And it's accusations like that I'm here to warn you against. I have plans to open a new clinic in the next few months. One that will help infertile couples. *Real couples.* Not FBI agents hell-bent on trying to ruin me and my reputation."

"Your own shady dealings ruined you," Kade fired back. "You used illegal immigrants as gestational carriers and surrogates. Hell, you didn't even pay them. Just room, board and minimal medical care." And for each of those women, McClendon and the clinic had collected plenty of money.

"Prove it," McClendon challenged.

"Give me time and I will. And while you're here, you could just go ahead and make a confession." Though Kade knew that wasn't going to happen.

McClendon looked ready to jump in with a smug answer, but instead, he pulled in a long breath. "I knew nothing about the illegal activity that went on." No more flexed eyebrows or surprise, feigned or otherwise. Fire went through McClendon's dust-gray eyes. "That was my son's doing and that idiot nurse, Jamie Greer. They'll be tried, and both will pay for their wrongdoings."

"Yes, they will," Kade assured him. "But that doesn't mean there won't be more charges. Ones that involve you spending a lot time in jail."

Now, the venom returned. "I'm not responsible for

those two losers' actions, and I refuse to have any of Anthony and Jamie's mud slung on me. Got that?"

McClendon didn't wait for Kade or Bree to respond to that. He turned and started off the porch.

"If you did this to Bree…to *us*," Kade corrected, calling out to the man. "I'll bring you down the hard way."

McClendon stopped and spared them a glance from over his shoulder. "Careful, Agent Ryland. You just might bite off more than you can chew. Trying to bring me down will be hazardous to your health. And anyone else who happens to get in my way."

Bree started after him, probably to rip him to shreds as Kade had wanted to do, but Kade caught her arm. She wasn't in any shape to take on a man like McClendon, and besides, assaulting an unarmed civilian wouldn't be good for the investigation.

And there would be an investigation.

That's how Kade could wipe that smug look off this rat's face. He didn't believe for one second that Mc-Clendon had stayed clean from all the illegal junk that went on at the clinic.

"An anonymous tipster," Bree mumbled. Her mind, too, was obviously on the investigation. Good. Because they needed answers and they needed them fast. That was the only way to make sure Leah remained safe.

Bree, too.

Even though Kade doubted she'd agree to let him protect her. Still, he had to do something to make things as safe as he could. McClendon had just thrown down the gauntlet, and it could be the start of another round of danger.

Kade's phone buzzed, and on the screen he could see it was from his brother, Dade. "Make sure McClendon leaves the grounds," Kade said to him as he watched the Jaguar speed away.

"I will," Dade assured. "But someone else is coming up the driveway. It's Dr. Mickelson, and he should be there any minute. Who's sick?"

Kade looked at Bree, who was still glaring at McClendon's retreating Jag, and he hoped that she didn't fall into that sick category. Heaven knows what her kidnappers had done to her these past ten and a half months. Hopefully nothing permanent, but he doubted they'd had her health and best interest at heart. There were a lot of nasty addictive drugs they could have used to force her to cooperate.

"The doc's here for Bree," Kade told his brother, and he ended the call just as he saw the doctor's vehicle approaching. Not a sleek luxury car. Dr. Mickelson was driving a blue pickup truck.

"This checkup is just for starters," Kade reminded Bree, just in case she planned to fight it. "Once we're sure Leah is safe, I want you at the hospital for a thorough exam."

She opened her mouth, probably to argue like he'd anticipated, but her fight was somewhat diminished by the dizzy glaze that came over her eyes. No doubt a residual effect of the drugs, or maybe crashing from the adrenaline that kept her going through the gunfight.

Kade caught her to keep her from falling. When she wobbled again, Kade cursed, holstered his gun and scooped her up in his arms.

Of course, she tried to wiggle out of his grip. "I'm not weak," Bree mumbled.

"You are now," Kade mumbled back. "Thanks for coming," he said to the doctor.

"This is Leah's birth mother?" the doctor asked.

Unlike their previous visitor, the doctor had concern all over his expression and in his body language. With his medical bag gripped in his hand, he hurried up the steps toward them.

"Yep, the birth mother," Kade verified.

The sterile title worked for him, but he didn't know if it would work for Bree. Especially not for long. He'd seen the way she had looked at Leah right before McClendon had interrupted them, and that was not the look of a *birth mother,* but rather a mother who loved her baby and had no plans to give her up.

"This way," Kade instructed the doctor, and he carried Bree up the stairs toward his living quarters.

There was probably a guest room clean and ready. There were three guest suites in the house, but Kade didn't want to take the time to call Bessie, the woman who managed the house. And she also managed the Rylands. Bessie was as close to a mother as he had these days. Heck, for most of his life, since his mother had passed away when he was barely eleven.

"I can walk," Bree insisted.

Kade ignored her again, used his boot to nudge open his door, and he walked through the sitting-office area to his bedroom. He deposited her on his king-size bed.

Funny, he'd thought about getting Bree into his bed from the moment he first met her on the undercover assignment, but he hadn't figured it would happen this way. Or ever. After Bree and he had escaped that clinic, he hadn't thought he would see her again. Now her life was permanently interlinked with his.

"She'll need blood drawn for a tox screen," Kade reminded Dr. Mickelson.

"Will do. Any possibility there's something going

on other than drugs?" the doctor asked. "Maybe an infection or something?"

Kade could only shake his head. "I'm not sure. She's been held captive for months. I have no idea what all they did to her. And neither does she."

"I'll run a couple of tests," Dr. Michelson assured him, and he motioned for Kade to wait outside.

That made sense, of course, because Dr. Mickelson would want to check Bree's C-section incision. Maybe other parts of her, too. Kade didn't want to be there for that, especially since Bree had already had her privacy violated in every way possible.

Kade eased the bedroom door shut, leaned against the wall. And waited. It didn't take long for the bad thoughts to fly right at him.

What the devil was he going to do?

McClendon's visit was a hard reminder that he hadn't left the danger at the motel in San Antonio. It could and maybe would follow them here to the ranch, the one place he considered safe.

He couldn't bear the thought of his baby girl being in harm's way, though she had been from the moment of her conception. What a heck of a way to start her life. But there was a silver lining in all of this. Leah was too young to know anything about her beginnings. She knew nothing of the danger.

Nothing of a mother who wasn't totally acting like a mother.

Yeah. That was unfair, and it caused Kade to wince a little. Bree needed to get her footing, and when she did…

Kade's thoughts went in a really bad direction.

When Bree got that inevitable footing, what if she wanted full custody of Leah? Until now, Kade hadn't thought beyond the next step of his investigation—and that step was to find Bree. Well, he'd found her all right.

Now what?

It sent a jab of fear through him to even consider it, but could he lose custody of his baby?

He shook his head. That couldn't happen. He wouldn't let it happen. Besides, Bree was a Jane and by her own admission not motherhood material. She worked impossible hours on assignments that sometimes lasted months. Then there was that whole confession about her being raised in foster care and never having planned to be a mother.

But Kade hadn't thought he was ready to be a father until he had seen Leah's face. Just the sight of her had caused something to switch in his head, and in that moment Leah became the most important person in his life.

He would die to protect his little girl. But his best chance of protecting Leah was to stay alive. And keep Bree alive, as well. There were probably some much-needed answers trapped in Bree's drug-hazed memories, and this exam by the doctor was the first step in retrieving those memories.

Kade's phone buzzed, and he saw on the screen that the call was from Mason. Mercy, he hoped nothing else had gone wrong. He'd had his *gone wrong* quota filled for the day.

"I've got news," Mason answered. As usual, there was no hint of emotion in his brother's voice. Mason definitely wasn't the sort of man to overreact, even when all hell was breaking loose. "I just got off the phone with Nate."

Kade breathed a little easier. Well, at first. Nate was handling the situation at the Treetop Motel in San Antonio where the gunman had tried to kill Bree and him. "Please tell me nothing's wrong," Kade commented.

"Not that I know of. But then all I got was a thirty-second update. Nate wanted me to tell you that he has his CSI folks out at the motel. They're going through the room where Bree was. His detectives also plan to comb the area to look for anyone who might have seen Bree come in."

That was a good start. "Any chance of surveillance cameras?"

"Slim to none. That neighborhood isn't big on that sort of thing."

Probably because it was a haven for drug dealers, prostitutes and a whole host of illegal activity. Still, they might get lucky. CSI could maybe find something that would help him identify Bree's kidnappers. That was step two. Then, once he had the culprits behind bars, he could think about this potential custody problem.

And Bree.

There was something stirring between them. Or maybe that was just lust or the uneasiness over what could turn out to be a potentially nasty custody dispute. Kade hoped that was all because lust and uneasiness were a lot easier to deal with than other things that could arise.

"I want to talk to Anthony McClendon and Jamie Greer again," Kade insisted. Both were suspects, just like Anthony's father, and he hadn't officially questioned them in months. "Can you set up the interviews and get them to the Silver Creek sheriff's office?"

That way, his brothers could assist, and he wouldn't have to be too far away from Leah or Bree. Though judging from her earlier behavior, Bree might want to get far away from here. He couldn't blame her after

McClendon's threats. The man hadn't named Leah specifically, but it had certainly sounded as if he were threatening the baby.

"Sure, I can get Anthony and Jamie out here. McClendon, too. But you have a couple of other fires to put out first. Special Agent Randy Cooper just called and demanded to see Bree. I take it he's her FBI handler or whatever it is you feds call your boss?"

"Yeah." Kade couldn't blame the man for wanting to see Bree, but the timing sucked.

"He seems kind of possessive if you ask me," Mason went on. "You sure he's just her handler?"

No. Kade wasn't sure of that. In fact, he didn't know if Leah had a boyfriend stashed somewhere. The only thing he knew about her was what he'd managed to read in her files. Which wasn't much. There wasn't a lot of paperwork and reports on undercover FBI Janes, and sometimes the files were nothing but cover fronts.

"Tell Coop he'll have to wait until tomorrow to see Bree," Kade said. "After the doctor finishes the exam, she'll need some rest."

That was the next step in his *for starters*. Maybe there wouldn't be anything that rest and time couldn't fix. Kade really needed her to recall more details of her captivity.

Mason made a sound of agreement. "Don't worry. I'll stall Coop." He paused. "Hold on a second. I just got a text from Nate. Might be important."

Kade could only hope this wasn't more bad news.

"There's another problem, little brother," Mason said. *"A big one."*

Chapter Six

Bree woke up to the sound of voices. Voices that she didn't immediately recognize.

She reached for her gun and phone. Not there. And an uneasy sense of déjà vu slammed through her. She sprang from the bed, her feet ready to start running when they landed on the thickly carpeted floor. Bree stopped cold.

Where the heck was she? And why hadn't there been a gun on the nightstand?

She glanced around the massive sun-washed bedroom, decorated in varying shades of blue and gray. At the king-size bed. The antique pine furniture. And it took her a moment to remember that she was at the Ryland ranch in Silver Creek.

More specifically, she'd been in Kade's bed.

She looked around again, first in the bathroom through the open door, then the massive dressing room. No sign of Kade.

So, she'd been in that bed alone.

And was apparently safe and sound since she had slept hard and long. After the ordeal she'd been through, she was thankful for that. Well, maybe. She was thankful *if* she hadn't missed anything important.

Which was possible.

After all, Leah was in her life now, and Kade and she were in the middle of a full-scale investigation. Yes, the potential for missing something important was sky-high, and she had to find Kade.

After she got dressed, that is.

Bree glanced down at the pink cotton pjs. They weren't familiar, either, but she did remember the doctor helping her change into them before he insisted that she sleep off the effects of the drugs her kidnapper had given her. She hadn't had a choice about that sleep, either. The fatigue and drugs had mixed with the adrenaline crash, and Bree hadn't been able to keep her eyes open at the end of the exam the doctor had given her.

Another glance, this time at the clock on the nightstand.

Oh, sheez.

It was nine, and she doubted that was p.m. because light was peeking through the curtains. It was nine in the morning, and that meant she'd been asleep at the ranch for heaven knows how many hours. Not good. She was certain she had plenty of things to do. But first, she needed to locate some clothes, the source of those voices and then see if she could scrounge up a phone and a strong cup of black coffee to clear the rest of the cobwebs from her head.

She hurried to the bathroom to wash up, but since she couldn't find a change of clothes, Bree gave up on the notion of getting dressed, and instead, she headed to the sitting room wearing the girlie pink pjs. She prayed nothing was wrong and that's why Kade had let her sleep so long. Too bad the thoughts of ugly scenarios kept going through her mind.

Bree threw open the door that separated the rooms in the suite and saw Kade. That was one voice. He was holding Leah and talking to someone. The other voice belonged to an attractive brunette that had her arm slung around Kade's waist.

The pang of jealousy hit Bree before she could see it coming.

"Oh," the woman said, her voice a classy purr.

Actually, everything about her was classy including her slim rose-colored top and skirt. Her hair was so shiny, so perfect, that Bree raked her hand through her own messy locks before she could stop herself. What was wrong with her? With everything else going on, the last thing she should care about was her appearance.

The woman smiled and walked toward her. "You must be Bree." Her smile stayed in place even when she eyed the pajamas. "I'm glad they fit."

"They're yours?" Bree asked.

The woman nodded.

Of course, they were. This woman was girlie, and she was also everything that Bree wasn't. Bree could see the love for her in Kade's eyes.

Another pang of jealousy.

Bree smoothed her hair down again before she could stop herself.

"I'm Darcy Ryland." The woman extended her hand for Bree to shake.

"Darcy is Nate's wife," Kade supplied. "He's the cop at SAPD who's helping us with the investigation."

Kade had a funny expression on his face as if he knew that Bree had been jealous.

Bree tossed him a scowl.

He gave her another funny look.

"I'm also the Silver Creek assistant D.A. and the mother of two toddlers who are waiting for me to bring them their favorite books and toys." Darcy checked her watch. "And that means I should have already been out of here. Good to meet you, Bree. We'll chat more when things settle down."

"Good to meet you, too," Bree mumbled.

Darcy tipped her head to the plush sofa. "I left you some other clothes—ones that aren't pink. Toiletries, too. And if you need anything else, just help yourself to my closet. Nate's and my quarters are in the west wing of the house. Just be careful not to trip over the toys if you go over there."

Bree added a thanks and felt guilty about the unflattering girlie thoughts and jealousy pangs. So, Kade's sister-in-law was, well, nice despite her picture-perfect looks.

Darcy walked back to Kade and picked up her purse from the table. In the same motion, she kissed him on the cheek and then kissed Leah. Using her purse, she waved goodbye to Bree and glided out of the room on gray heels that looked like torture devices to Bree.

Bree didn't waste any time going to Leah. No blanket this morning. The baby was wearing a one-piece green outfit that was nearly the same color as her eyes. She was also wide-awake and had those eyes aimed at Kade. Leah seemed to be studying his every move.

"I slept too long," Bree commented, and she touched her fingers to Leah's cheek. The baby automatically turned in her direction. "You should have woken me up sooner."

Bree wondered if there was a time when that wouldn't seem like such a huge deal. She hoped not. Because now everything seemed like a miracle, and just looking at her baby washed away all her dark thoughts and mood.

"You needed sleep," Kade insisted.

When he didn't continue, Bree looked up at him.

And she waited. Clearly, he had something on his mind, and thankfully he didn't make her wait long to deliver the news.

"The doctor got back your lab results."

That hung in the air like deadweight. Bree couldn't speak, couldn't ask the question that put her breath in a vise—had the drugs permanently harmed Leah or her?

"You had a large amount of Valium in your system. It caused the grogginess and the temporary memory loss." He paused. "It was temporary, right?"

She nodded and felt relief. Well, partly. "Any chance they gave me Valium when I was pregnant?"

"It's hard to tell, but Leah is perfectly healthy," Kade assured her. "I suspect because they wanted to use the baby for leverage that they didn't do anything that would risk harming her."

Good. That was something, at least. And with that concern out of the way, Bree could turn her full attention back to Leah.

"The doctor said any gaps in your memory should return," Kade explained. "So, it's possible you'll remember other details about your kidnappers."

She had a dozen or more questions to ask Kade about the test results and an update on the case, but Bree couldn't get her attention off Leah. She had to be the most beautiful baby ever born.

Or else Bree's brain had turned to mush.

"How is she this morning?" Bree asked.

"Fine. She just had her bottle." He motioned toward the empty one on the table.

She felt a pang of a different kind. Bree wished she'd been awake to feed her, and she cursed the long sleep session that had caused her to miss all these incredible moments.

"How long before she'll want another bottle?" Bree asked.

"Around one or two." He paused again. "There's a problem," Kade said.

Bree's gaze flew to his because she thought he was going to say that something was wrong with Leah, after all. She held her breath, praying it wasn't that.

"Late yesterday, Nate's detectives at SAPD found the gunman who shot at us," Kade finished. "He's dead."

Bree groaned. So, the problem wasn't with Leah, but it was still a big one.

"Please tell me he managed to make a confession before he died?" Bree asked.

"Afraid not. His name was Clyde Cummings. We ID'd him from his prints since he had a long rap sheet. In and out of trouble with the law most of his life." Another pause. "Word on the street is he was a hired gun."

That didn't surprise Bree. Whoever had masterminded her kidnapping had no doubt hired this goon. A goon who would have succeeded in killing her if Kade hadn't arrived in time to save her.

"Cummings didn't die in a shoot-out with the cops," Kade continued. "When Nate's men found him, he was already dead." Kade paused again. "He died from a single gunshot wound to the back of the head."

Oh, mercy. An execution-style hit on a hit man. That meant someone didn't want Cummings talking to the cops, or maybe this had been punishment for allowing Kade and her to get away. It didn't matter which. The bottom line was this case was far from being over.

Bree looked at Leah and hated that Kade and she had to have a conversation like this in front of her. A baby deserved better, even if Leah was too young to know what they were saying. Still, she might be able to sense the tension in the room. Bree could certainly feel it, and it had her stomach turning and twisting.

"Since we don't know who hired Cummings," Kade went on, "my sisters-in-law and the kids are leaving town for a while. Darcy came back to pack some things."

That gave Bree something else to be frustrated about. The monster after her had now managed to disrupt the entire Ryland family. Now, all of them were in possible danger, and that included Kade's nephews and niece.

Kade ducked down a little so that they were eye to eye. "I think it's a good idea if Leah goes with Darcy and the others."

"No," flew out of her mouth before Bree could stop it. But she immediately hated her response and hated even more that she might have to take it back.

"I'm just getting to know her," Bree mumbled, and she kissed Leah's cheek as she'd seen Kade do. Each kiss, each moment was a gift that she didn't deserve but would take, anyway.

Bree pulled in a long breath and tried to push away the ache. But no, it was still there. It hurt her to the core to think of her daughter being whisked away when she'd only had a few real moments with her. It hurt even more though to know that Leah was in danger and would continue to be until Kade and she put an end to it.

"Whoever killed Cummings could hire someone else," Bree said, more to herself than Kade. She had to make her heart understand what her brain and instincts already knew. Her training and experience forced her to see scenarios and outcomes that ripped away at her.

"Just where exactly is this safe place that the others and Leah could go?" she asked.

"My other sister-in-law, Kayla, has a house in San

Antonio. It's an estate with a high wrought-iron fence and security system surrounding the entire grounds and house. SAPD will provide additional protection. Plus, Dade and Nate would be with them."

It sounded like a fortress. Ideal for keeping her baby safe. But Bree knew that bad guys might still try to get through all those security measures.

"You could go, too," Kade quietly added.

"No." And this time, Bree wouldn't take back her response. Just the opposite. It was the only answer that made sense. "Wherever I go, the danger will follow. I'm the one this person wants dead, and I don't want Leah anywhere around if and when he hires another hit man to come after me."

Kade didn't argue. Because he knew it was the truth. The more distance between her baby and her, the better.

Still, that didn't ease the ache that was quickly turning into a raw, throbbing pain.

"This is much harder than I thought it would be," Bree whispered.

Kade only nodded, and she could see the agony in his icy gray eyes. So much emotion that it prompted Bree to touch her fingertips to his arm. She wasn't big on providing comfort, and her job had required her not to sympathize with anything or anybody, but she and Kade shared this heartbreak.

"When would Leah have to go to Kayla's house?" she asked.

Kade lifted his shoulder and sank down on the sofa. "Soon. This morning," he clarified. "But maybe it wouldn't be for long."

Maybe.

And maybe it would be far longer than Bree's heart could handle.

An uncomfortable silence settled between them, and Bree eased down on the sofa right next to him. She waited. Hoping. And it wasn't long before Kade sighed and placed the baby in her arms.

It was far better than anything else he could have done.

It soothed her. And frightened her. It filled her with a hundred emotions that she didn't understand. But even that seemed trivial.

She was holding her baby.

And it was breaking her into pieces.

Until this moment she hadn't realized she could love someone this much. Or hurt this much because she might lose her, even for only a day or two.

"What are we going to do?" Bree said under her breath.

When Kade didn't answer, she looked at him and saw his jaw muscles set in iron.

Handsome iron, she amended.

Because his good looks weren't diminished by a surly expression or the possible impending danger. Again, she blamed it on their shared situation. And on the close contact between them. After all, they were arm to arm. Hip to hip. Breath to breath. Except she doubted Kade was thinking about the close contact in a good way.

That expression let her know that he hadn't told her everything, and the part that he had left out would be something that would only add to the pain she was already feeling.

"Okay, what's wrong?" Bree demanded.

He didn't answer right away. He'd mulled over his answer. "I'm not giving up Leah."

For a moment she thought he meant that he'd changed

his mind about the baby going to the San Antonio estate, but then she got it.

Oh, yeah.

She got it all right.

Kade had physical custody of Leah since she was just a few days old. Plus, he had something that Bree didn't—a home, a supportive family and money from the looks of it. There was also the fact that he had strong ties in the community. That meant ties with people who could help him keep custody of their child.

Still, that was just one side of it.

"I'm her mother," Bree said when she couldn't think of another argument. It certainly wasn't a good one, and it didn't mean she had what it took to raise a child. But the other side was that she loved this child with all her heart.

Kade nodded. "And I'm her father."

Frustrated, she stared at him. "Does this mean we're at some kind of stalemate?"

"No." And that's all he said for several moments. "It means we have some things to work out. Things that will be in Leah's best interest."

Bree could see where this was going, and she didn't like the direction one bit. "You think you can be a better parent than me."

He didn't deny it.

She couldn't deny it, either. He certainly looked at ease with Leah. So did the other members of his family that she'd met. Leah was a Ryland.

But she was Bree's baby, too.

Bree huffed. "I'm not just giving her up, either." Even though it didn't make logical sense, it made sense to her. As a mother. Yes, it was a new role, new feelings.

New everything. But it was a role she would embrace with as much devotion and love as she had her badge.

Kade didn't huff, but he mumbled something under his breath. "Be reasonable about this. You're a Jane for heaven's sake."

Bree jumped right on that. "And I could become a regular agent. Like you."

In the past that would have caused her to wince. Or laugh because she had thought a regular job would be a boring death sentence. But she wasn't wincing or laughing now. In fact, she was on the verge of crying at the thought of losing this child that she hardly knew.

With those iron jaw muscles still in place, Kade leaned forward and picked up the little silver object from the table. Bree recognized the design. It was the same as the tattoo on his shoulder. He began to roll it like a coin across his fingers. Maybe as a stress reliever. Maybe so he wouldn't have to look at her. Whatever, it was working.

Well, for Kade.

Bree didn't think anything could relieve her stress, but she shoved that aside and tried to reach a solution. Even a temporary one. She sure needed something to get her through this morning.

"We only have a few hours to spend with Leah before she leaves," Bree conceded. "We can table this discussion until after...well, after," she settled for saying.

Because she refused to admit this could end badly. The stakes were too high for that.

"Later, then," Kade agreed, and he looked back at her. His expression let her know that *later, then,* wasn't going to happen immediately.

"There aren't a lot of rules for situations like this. And we don't know each other very well." He kept rolling the concho. "In fact, I don't know much about you at all."

It wasn't a gruff or barked observation. It was conversation, that's all, and he had genuine concern in his voice. Bree knew this could turn ugly, but since he was trying to make nice, she tried, too.

"Bree is my real name. Bree Ann Winston. I'm twenty-nine." She paused. Frowned. "Wait. What's the date?"

He glanced at his watch. "June 14."

That required a deep breath. "Okay, I'm thirty." She'd missed a pivotal birthday by two months.

Ironically, it had been a birthday that she'd been dreading since many Janes didn't last long after their mid-thirties. They were either dead or moved to a regular agent position. However, after the ordeal she'd just been through, turning thirty didn't seem so bad, after all.

"Both of my parents are dead," she continued, addressing another touchy subject. "They were killed in a meth lab explosion when I was nine. Let's just say they weren't stellar parents and leave it at that. I spent the rest of my so-called childhood in foster care."

Hellish foster care that she didn't discuss. Ever. With anyone.

Bree took another deep breath. She hadn't intended to confess all of that dirty laundry, but she figured this wasn't a good time to keep secrets. Besides, if it came down to a custody fight with Kade, he'd find out, anyway. Kade would learn that prior to becoming an FBI agent, she'd been a mess. A juvenile record for underage drinking. Truancy. And running away from foster care. Especially that. Bree had lost count of how many times she'd run. In fact, she always ran when things got tough.

Or rather she had.

She wouldn't run now.

"So, there's the dirt on me," she concluded. "Nothing like your life, I'm sure."

He made a sound that could have meant anything and followed it with a deep breath to indicate it was his turn to spill his guts. "I'm Kade Jason Ryland. Age thirty-one. And I've lived here at this ranch my entire life. Wouldn't want to live anywhere else."

She could see him here as a little boy. Learning to ride those magnificent horses that she'd seen in the painting in the foyer. Running through this sprawling house surrounded by older brothers and other family who loved him the way Bree loved Leah. It was so far from what she'd experienced as a kid that it seemed like a fantasy.

Kade's next deep breath came with a change of expression. His forehead bunched up, and he dodged her gaze. "When I was ten, my grandfather was murdered. He was the sheriff then, and well, I was close to him. All of us were. He was gunned down by an unknown assailant, and the case has never been solved."

"I'm sorry." And that was genuine. An injustice like that ate away at you. Obviously, that's what it'd done to Kade. She could see the hurt still there in his eyes.

He shrugged, and she saw the shield come down. He was guarding himself now. Bree knew, because she was a master of doing it.

"A few days after my grandfather was murdered, my father gave me and my five brothers a custom-made silver concho." He held it up for her to see.

"That was nice of him." Though there was something about his tone that said differently.

"It was a guilt gift." Kade didn't continue until he'd

taken Leah from her and put the baby in the carrier seat on the table in front of them. "After that, my father walked out on us. My mother killed herself because she was severely depressed, and my older brother, Grayson, had to forgo college, life and everything else so he could raise all of us and keep the ranch going."

Kade met her gaze. "So, there's the dirt on me."

Okay. Bree hadn't expected anything other than a fairy tale family story to do with the idyllic family ranch, but that was more a nightmare. The sympathy came, and it didn't feel as foreign to her as she thought it would.

"I'm sorry," she repeated.

He waved her off. "Yeah. I'm sorry about your life, too."

It was the first time she ever remembered anyone saying that and really meaning it. And much to her surprise, it felt good. Too good. And it set off more warnings in her head. Her motto of *don't trust anyone* was slowly being chipped away.

By Kade.

She looked up at him, to thank him, not just for the reciprocal sympathy but also for taking care of their baby when she hadn't been around to do it.

Kade looked at her, too. And her *thank you* died on her lips when he put his arms around her and pulled her to him.

"We have to be together on this," he whispered.

It wasn't exactly the kiss that she'd braced herself for. Just the opposite. He was holding her as if trying to comfort her.

His arms were warm and strong. So welcoming. Of course, she'd been in his arms before at the fertility clinic. She'd been naked then. Kade had, too. And his body had definitely given her dreams and food for thought.

Not now, of course.

And Bree wanted to believe that.

Too bad those memories warmed her far more than they should have. It'd been a job, she reminded herself. And that job was over now. Kade's naked body was just a memory, and it had to stay that way.

Bree wanted to believe that, too.

He pulled back, met her gaze. His breath was warm, as well, and he moved closer. Closer. Until his mouth brushed against hers. Bree tried to brace herself again, but what she didn't do was move away.

"I'd kiss you," he drawled, "but we both know that'd be a bad idea."

She was about to agree with him, but Kade leaned in and touched his mouth to hers again. Still not a kiss, but it heated her as thoroughly as if it had been one.

"A bad idea," she repeated. Mercy. She sounded like a wimp. And she still wasn't moving. Bree could see what was happening. Like a big train wreck. Except this was a wreck that her body was aching to experience.

What would a real kiss feel like with Kade?

The fake ones had been amazingly potent, and she figured a real one would pretty much melt her into a puddle.

"Bad," he mumbled without taking his eyes off her.

Bree could see a kiss coming. Could feel it. And she heard herself say *uh-oh* a split second before Kade snapped away from her.

Okay.

No kiss, after all. She didn't know who looked more disappointed or more confused—Kade or her.

He cursed. Some really bad words. And Bree thought

that was it. The end of the possible lethal kiss. But then
he came back at her. He grabbed her and put his mouth
on hers. And it wasn't for just a peck this time.

This was a Kade Ryland kiss.

Yes, this was so different from the fake ones, and
they weren't even naked to enjoy the full benefits. Still,
there were benefits. His mouth moved over hers as if
he'd been born to kiss her like this.

The heat washed through her, head to toe. It cleared
the haze and fogginess from her mind while it created
some haze of a different kind. Her body was suddenly
on fire.

From one blasted kiss!

How could he do that to her body? How could he dis-
solve all her defenses and make her want him like this?

Bree wasn't sure she wanted to know the answer. But
she was certain that she wanted the kiss to continue.
And it couldn't. For one thing, Leah was in the room.
For another, neither Kade nor she was in a good place
for this to be happening.

Still, she wasn't the one to stop. Kade did. Later,
much later, after her body cooled down, she might actually thank him for it.

He pulled back, dragged his tongue over his bottom lip and made a sound of approval. Or something.
Whatever the sound, it went through her as fiery hot
as the kiss.

Bree didn't ask for clarification on what that sound
meant. She didn't need it. That kiss had held up to the
fantasies she'd had after those naked fake kisses at the
clinic.

"I'm sorry," Kade said.

She didn't have time to repeat that lie to him because
someone cleared their throat and both Bree and Kade

turned toward the open doorway. It was Mason, and he obviously hadn't missed the close contact between them. He didn't look too pleased about it, either, but then he hadn't looked pleased about much since her arrival.

"You got a visitor," Mason said, his attention landing on her. "SA Randy Cooper."

Coop. The very person that she should have called by now. Sheez. How could she have forgotten that? But then Bree remembered.

Sleep, baby and kisses.

Yes. That had really eaten into her time, but she had to get her mind back on track. She had to think like an agent because that was the best way to keep her baby safe.

"I had him wait on the front porch," Mason explained. "Just in case you didn't want to see him."

Oh, she wanted to see him all right. She turned to Kade. "I need to change my clothes. Best if I don't talk to my boss while wearing these pink pjs."

He nodded and picked up Leah in the infant carrier. "Mason can watch Leah. Meet me downstairs in the living room after you've changed."

"There's more," Mason said, and that stopped both Kade and her midstep. "Somebody else called the sheriff's office and left a message for you. And it's a call I think you'll need to return before you speak to Agent Cooper."

Bree shook her head, not understanding that remark. "Who wants to talk to us?" she asked cautiously.

"To *you*," Mason corrected, staring right at her. "It's Anthony McClendon."

One of their suspects. She glanced at Kade, wondering if he knew why Anthony would be calling her, but he only lifted his shoulder.

"What does he want?" Kade demanded.

"Apparently a lot. He's either lying through his teeth or else you should rethink seeing Agent Cooper. That's why I left him on the porch and locked the front door. I reset the security alarm, too."

Bree lifted her shoulders. "Why would you take those kinds of measures for a federal officer?" she added. "And why would you listen to a piece of scum like Anthony McClendon?"

It was Mason's turn to shrug. "Because he says he has proof that Cooper is dirty."

"Proof?" Kade challenged.

Mason nodded. "Oh, yeah. And he says he's also got evidence that Cooper is the one who wants Bree dead."

Chapter Seven

"Proof," Kade mumbled while he waited for Bree to change her clothes.

He was eager to hear exactly what that would be or if such a thing even existed. Kade had already tried to return Anthony's call, but it had gone straight to voice mail.

"So-called proof coming from a confirmed suspect awaiting trial," Mason interjected. He dropped down on the sofa and gave Leah's foot a little wiggle. His brother didn't smile, but it was as close to a loving expression as Mason ever managed. "Anthony could be just blowing smoke."

Under normal circumstances that reminder would have been enough to calm some of Kade's concerns. But it wasn't enough now.

His daughter was in the house.

The very house that Coop was waiting to get inside. Yeah, Mason would protect Leah, and Kade could do the same to Bree, but he hated the possibility of danger being so close. Bree already had enough danger dumped on her, and judging from her still-sleepy eyes and unfocused expression, she wasn't anywhere near ready to face down someone who might not be on their side.

Especially when it was someone she thought was on their side.

"I'm ready," Bree announced, hurrying out of the bathroom. No more cotton candy pajamas. She wore loose black pants and a pale purple top. Darcy's colors. But they didn't look so bad on Bree, either.

Kade also saw the change in her body language. No more lack of focus. Hers was the expression of an agent who wanted some answers. Or maybe she just wanted to throttle Anthony for making that accusation against her boss.

"I know, I know," she mumbled when she followed his gaze. She went to Leah and kissed her forehead. "The clothes aren't my usual style."

"You look good," he settled for saying.

Bree glanced down at the outfit and grumbled a distracted thanks. Her mind was obviously locked on seeing their visitor.

Kade aimed for the same mind lock. He pushed her clothes, Leah, the kiss and this attraction for her aside so he could deal with something potentially dangerous.

"You trust Coop?" he came right out and asked.

"Of course." She answered without hesitation, but she stopped on her way to the door. Now, she paused and shook her head. *"Of course,"* she repeated it and slowly turned back around to face him. "What did Anthony have to say about Coop wanting me dead?"

"I wasn't able to reach him, but I left a message and told him to call my cell."

"Well, I'm sure whatever comes from Anthony's mouth will be a lie," she added and headed out of the room. "Coop's not the enemy. I can't say the same for Anthony, especially since he's facing criminal charges."

Kade hoped she was right about Coop, but just in

case, he kept his hand over his gun. He also moved ahead of Bree, hoping that he could keep himself between Coop and her until he could determine if there was a shred of truth to Anthony's allegations.

The maneuver earned him a huff from Bree.

He gave her a huff right back.

Kade disarmed the security system and looked out the side window. It was Coop all right. Kade had had many conversations with the lanky blond-haired man while he'd been searching for Bree. Conversations where Kade had been sure that Coop's actions were the right ones.

He hoped he continued to feel that way when he opened the door.

"Bree," Coop said on a rise of breath as if he truly hadn't expected to see her. The man stepped forward, and Kade had to make a split-second decision about letting him in.

But Bree made the decision for him. She stepped around Kade and pulled Coop into her arms for a hug. The man hugged back and kept repeating her name. It was a regular warm and fuzzy reunion.

"I never thought I'd see you again," Coop whispered, though it was plenty loud enough for Kade to hear.

"It was touch-and-go yesterday," Kade offered.

"Yes." Coop eased away from Bree and had the decency to look a little uncomfortable with his public display of affection for his subordinate.

Coop then turned his attention to Kade. "I heard about the shooting in San Antonio. About the dead gunman, too. You should have called me the second you got that anonymous tip."

That would have been protocol, yes, but Kade hadn't exactly been operating on a logical level. "No time for calls," Kade answered. "As it was, I barely had time to get her out of there alive."

Coop still seemed annoyed that he hadn't been looped in. "Thanks for getting her out."

"I didn't do it for you." Kade should have probably kept that to himself, but there was something about this reunion that riled him. Hopefully, it was Anthony's accusation and not the possessive way Coop was holding on to Bree.

Coop took something from his pocket and handed it to her. Her badge. Bree closed her fingers around it, then slipped it into her pocket. "Thanks."

"I got it from your apartment after you went missing," Coop explained. "I figured you'd want it back right away. You always said you felt naked without it."

Coop smiled.

Kade didn't.

And he hated that at a critical time like this the naked comment had an effect on him. A bad one. The kiss had been a huge mistake, and worse, he wanted to make that mistake again. He hoped he didn't feel that way because of the shot of jealousy he'd just experienced.

"I talked to the doctor who examined you," Coop volunteered, dropping the smile. "He wouldn't tell me much, other than you were okay. He did say there'd be no lasting complications from the delivery or your ordeal."

"Other than the threat to her life," Kade spoke up. He looked at Bree to give her a chance to ask Coop about what was on both their minds.

She flexed her eyebrows and sucked in a quick breath. "Anthony McClendon called the ranch. He made some, uh, accusations against you."

Coop's eyes widened, and he tossed his concerned

gaze first to Kade and then back to Bree. "What kind of accusations?"

"Anthony said you were *dirty*," Bree explained, then paused. "And that you're the one who's trying to kill me." She waved it off before he could say anything. "He's lying, of course."

"But he said he had proof," Kade added.

"Then he's lying about that, too," Coop said as gospel.

Coop caught Bree's arm and turned her to face him. "Anthony's guilty of a lot of things that went on at the Fulbright clinic. It was pure luck on his part that we didn't get those missing surveillance backups that would have no doubt proven that he's guilty of even more serious charges. If he's trying to put a spin on this, it's because he knows I'm going to put his sorry butt in jail."

Kade agreed that Anthony was likely guilty of something more than harboring illegal immigrants, theft and embezzlement, but he still wanted to hear what the man had to say. Especially what he had to say about Coop.

"What's the status of the Fulbright investigation?" Bree asked.

"It's still active," Coop said. "Kade and you gave us a good start with your undercover work, and I'm still digging. Trying to connect the dots. I do know that Anthony was skimming money from the clinic, and that's why father and son are now at odds."

Kade had learned the same thing, but realized that he hadn't brought Bree up to speed on the case. Of course, there hadn't been much time for that between dodging bullets and sleeping off the Valium.

"And what about the shooting yesterday?" Bree

pressed. "Any word on who might have hired a hit man to come after me?"

"Nothing yet. It's SAPD's jurisdiction. For now. But I've requested that the FBI take over, since the shots were fired at two agents."

Yeah, but moving it to the FBI would take Nate out of the investigative loop. Kade preferred his brother in on this. Nate had an objective eye, and Kade needed that right now. Clearly, his objectivity had taken a hike. First the kiss. Now the jealousy.

He wasn't on a good track here.

Bree blew out a long, weary breath. "Is there any evidence about why someone would have kidnapped me in the first place?"

Coop shook his head and gave her arm a gentle squeeze. "I'm sorry. I'm trying hard, but I haven't been able to prove anything. Of course, my theory is that McClendon did all of this so he'd have some leverage over the investigation."

"But he hasn't contacted Bree, me or you to try to tamper with evidence or anything." Kade tried not to make it sound like a question. He also tried not to be so suspicious of a fellow agent.

Oh, man. He couldn't let a suspect like Anthony play these kinds of mind games.

"McClendon hasn't contacted me *yet*," Coop verified. "I figured it would happen as Anthony's and Jamie's trial dates got closer. But since Bree managed to escape and since the baby is here and safe, the person responsible has lost their leverage."

Kade wanted to believe that, because if it were true, then that meant the danger to Bree and Leah had lessened. Well, maybe. That didn't mean the person wouldn't try to kidnap them again. But at least both were safe now.

And it had to stay that way.

Even if he had to check out Anthony's crazy allegation. Kade would do that and anything else that it took. He made a mental note to recheck all the security measures at the ranch. And to try to convince Bree to take him up on his offer to send her to a safe house.

"So, what are your immediate plans?" Coop asked Bree. But he didn't wait for her to answer that. "How soon are you returning to work?"

She glanced at Kade, and he was certain that he looked as surprised as she did. The timing was all off, but Kade didn't jump to answer for her.

"I'm not sure," she finally said. Not an answer, but it appeared that was all she was going to give him. She fluttered her hand toward the stairs. "I want to spend some time with my daughter. Get to know her."

Coop's forehead bunched up. "I thought you'd want to figure out who kidnapped you right away."

"I will." But then she paused. "I just need some time."

Coop's gaze shifted to Kade, and the man instantly frowned. "Not too much time, I hope. Bree, you haven't worked in nearly a year."

"That wasn't exactly her fault," Kade pointed out.

Coop's frown deepened, and he moved even closer to Bree. "Officially, you were listed as missing in the line of duty, but we both know your Jane identity was compromised when things went wrong at the Fulbright clinic. Your face was on those surveillance videos, and your cover was blown."

Kade couldn't deny any of that. But what he still didn't know was how their cover had been blown. It was definitely something he wanted to learn, but for now, he had other things that were much higher priority.

"What are you saying?" Bree asked Coop. "That I can no longer be a Jane? Well, that's okay. It would have been hard to pull off deep-cover assignments now that I have Leah."

Coop looked as if she'd slugged him. "I didn't think you'd ever give that up without a fight." He shook his head and stared at her as if she'd lost her mind. Or as if Kade had brainwashed her. "But that's not the only problem we have here. Bree, there are people in the Justice Department who feel you brought this kidnapping on yourself. That you didn't take the proper security precautions."

Kade tamped down the rush of anger and stepped by Bree's side. "They're blaming the victim?"

Coop huffed. "No. I'm not saying that—"

But he didn't get to finish because Mason appeared at the top of the stairs. He had Leah's carrier in his left hand, and he had the baby positioned behind him in a protective stance.

"We have another problem," Mason called down to Kade. "The ranch hand that I've got watching the security cameras just called, and we have some more visitors. He's running the plates, but it looks like Anthony McClendon and Jamie Greer."

"Good," Coop spat out, and he drew his gun. "Because I can confront the SOB about the lies he's spreading about me."

Kade look at Bree, and her expression verified how he felt. This wasn't *good*. Far from it. Two of their suspects were way too close for comfort, and they had a riled agent with his gun drawn.

"Keep your gun down," Kade ordered Coop. "And

you need to stay with Leah," he added to his brother. "Call a couple of the ranch hands to the front in case I need backup."

"I'm your backup," Coop snarled, and with his gun ready, he stormed out onto the porch.

Kade caught Bree's arm to stop her from following. "I know you won't wait upstairs with Mason." He reached down and pulled the Colt .38 from his ankle holster. Kade had no idea if she had a steady aim yet, but even if she didn't, he preferred Bree to be armed.

"Thanks," she mumbled, but her attention was on the stairs where Mason had just left with Leah. "He's a good cop?" she asked.

"Yeah. And we're not letting anyone get past us."

She nodded, licked her lips and looked a little shakier than Kade wanted. However, he couldn't take the time to soothe her because he didn't want bullets to start flying this close to Leah. Even though Coop was a well-trained agent, he seemed to be working on a short fuse when it came to Anthony.

Kade stepped onto the porch, with Bree behind him, just as the white Lexus stopped next to Coop's car. It was Anthony and Jamie all right. Kade had interviewed them enough to recognize them from a distance.

Anthony got out first. He definitely didn't look like a killer or even a formidable opponent. The man was lanky to the point of being skinny, and his black hair was pretty thin for a man in his early thirties. But Kade knew that Anthony had some strength. During their undercover assignment, Kade had watched Anthony get into a shoving match with an irate illegal immigrant father who was looking for his daughter. Anthony had some martial arts skills to make up for all that lankiness.

The man wore no scrubs today, as he'd worn in all his interviews with Kade. He was dressed in khakis and a white shirt. He looked like a nerd. If he was carrying a concealed weapon, Kade didn't see any signs of it. That didn't mean Kade would let down his guard. Neither would Coop. Or Bree.

"No reason for those guns," Anthony called out. "I'm just here to talk."

"You mean you're here to lie," Coop shouted back.

Oh, yeah. This could turn ugly fast, and Kade was thankful when he spotted the three armed ranch hands round the east corner of the house. The men stopped Anthony in his tracks, probably because they were armed with rifles that no amount of martial arts could match.

But those rifles didn't stop Jamie from getting out of the car.

Jamie spared the ranch hands a cool, indifferent glance before she slid on a pair of dark sunglasses and strolled toward them as if this were a planned social visit. No nerd status for her. Jamie was tall and lean, and she had her long auburn hair gathered into a sleek ponytail. Kade had always thought Jamie looked more like a socialite than a nurse.

"How did you know I was here?" Coop demanded.

"I didn't." Anthony looked past him and put his attention on Bree. "I came here to see you. It's all over the news about the shooting, and since Agent Ryland wasn't at his office in San Antonio, I thought he might bring you here. Obviously, I guessed right."

Kade hoped it was a guess, and that Anthony didn't have any insider knowledge. Of course, Anthony could have learned Bree's location from his father, but Kade didn't think the two were on speaking terms.

"Why'd you want to see Bree?" Kade demanded while Anthony and Coop started another glaring contest with each other.

"Because SAPD has been hassling us again," Jamie calmly provided. "And Anthony and I thought we'd better nip this in the bud."

"What are you planning to nip?" Kade asked, and he didn't bother trying to sound friendly. He wanted all three of these people off his porch and off his family's property.

"You, if necessary." Jamie turned toward Kade, though with those dark shades, he couldn't tell exactly where she was looking. "You had your shot at investigating us, and you found nothing on me other than a few charges that you can't make stick."

"Not yet. But at least you'll do some time in jail. That'll be enough for now." Kade knew it sounded like a threat, and he was glad of it. "Bree's been through hell and back, and someone will pay for that."

Anthony pointed toward Coop. "What about him? He should be the one paying."

"I warned you about those lies." There was a dark, dangerous edge to Coop's voice.

Still, Anthony came closer, but he pleaded his case to Bree, not Coop or Kade. "Did Agent Cooper tell you that he provided *security* to the Fulbright clinic and that he was paid a hefty amount for his services?"

"Security?" Kade repeated over Coop's profanity-punctuated shouts that this was all a crock.

Anthony nodded, and Jamie strolled closer until she was near the bottom step and standing next to Anthony. "It's true. Anthony's father told me that Agent Cooper kept the local cops from digging too deeply into what was going on."

Coop turned that profanity tirade to Jamie, but it didn't stop the woman from continuing.

"Hector said Cooper was stunned when he realized Bree, one of his own agents, had been sneaked into the undercover assignment at the clinic that could ultimately land him in jail." Jamie paused, a trace of a smile on her dark red lips. "And Anthony here has proof."

Anthony had a bit of a smile going on, as well. Kade could understand why—*if* there was proof. And it was that possibility of proof that kept Kade from latching onto them and giving them the boot.

"Anthony and you have nothing on me," Coop fired back. "Neither does Hector McClendon."

But Jamie only shrugged. "You're investigating the wrong people, Agent Ryland. You need to be looking closer to home. You need to investigate Agent Cooper."

Bree huffed and stepped around Kade, between Coop and him. But she didn't say anything. She just studied Jamie from head to toe, and Kade had to wait just like the others to hear Bree's take on all of this.

"Are you the woman who held me captive all those months?" Bree asked.

With all the other accusations flying around about Coop, Kade certainly hadn't expected such a direct question from Bree. But he waited for Jamie's answer and watched her expression. He wished he could strip those glasses off her so he could see her eyes because he was certain that question had hit some kind of nerve.

Jamie shifted her posture and folded her arms over her chest. "I did nothing wrong," she insisted.

Kade looked at Bree to see if she believed Jamie, but Bree only shook her head. It made sense. After all, Bree had said her kidnappers had kept on prosthetic masks, but he'd hoped that she would recognize something about Jamie or Anthony.

Of course, maybe there was nothing to recognize because they hadn't been the ones to hold her captive.

"Did. You. Hold. Me. Captive?" Bree repeated. Her anger came through loud and clear.

Jamie shifted again. "No." She paused. "Are you accusing me so you can protect your boss? My advice? Don't. Because accusing me won't do anything for your safety. Or your baby's safety." Jamie leaned in and lowered her voice as if telling a secret. "Investigate him, and you'll learn the truth, even if it's not what you want to hear."

That got Coop started again. "I want to see this so-called proof of my guilt," Coop demanded.

Anthony lifted his hands, palms up. "You think I'm stupid enough to bring it with me? *Right.* Then you just kill me and take it."

"I'm an FBI agent," Coop fired back, "and I'm not in the habit of killing people just because they're telling lies about me."

"I'm not lying, and you know it." Anthony turned to Kade and Bree. "I have an eyewitness who'll testify that Agent Cooper here had a meeting with my father at the clinic, less than an hour before your cover was blown."

Oh, that was not what Kade wanted to hear, and by God, it had better not be true. If so, Coop would pay and pay hard.

"That witness will also tell you that Cooper took money from my father," Anthony smugly added.

It took a moment for Kade to get his teeth unclenched. Bree had a similar reaction. She was hurling daggers at Anthony with a cold glare, but she wasn't exactly giving Coop a resounding vote of confidence, either.

"Sounds like I need to talk to this witness," Bree commented.

"No, you don't." Coop walked toward Jamie and Anthony with his finger pointing at the man who'd just accused him of assorted felonies. "I'm not going to let you get away with this."

Because Kade didn't want Coop to do something they'd both regret, he grabbed his fellow agent. He held on until he was sure Coop would stay put.

"We're not dealing with this here at the ranch," Kade informed Anthony, Jamie and Coop. He shifted his attention to Anthony. "Bring the witness to the Silver Creek sheriff's office. And while you're at it, both of you come prepared to answer some more questions because this investigation is just getting started."

Jamie groaned softly and mumbled something. "I've had enough questions to last me a lifetime."

Kade tossed her a glare. "Then you'll get a few more. Be there when Anthony brings in this secret witness."

Much to Kade's surprise, Anthony nodded, and his smile wasn't so little now. The man was smirking when he headed back to his car. "Come on, Jamie. We're finished here, for the moment."

But Jamie paused a moment and glanced over her shoulder at Anthony before she spoke. "I don't trust Anthony," she said in a whisper. "And neither should you. The man is dangerous."

Bree and Kade exchanged a glance, and she was no doubt thinking the same thing—what the heck was this all about? One minute ago Jamie had been ice-cold and unruffled. Now she looked on the verge of panicking.

"If Anthony is dangerous, then why did you come here with him?" Bree asked.

Jamie didn't answer right away. She glanced over her shoulder again as if to make sure Anthony wasn't close enough to hear. "Because sometimes the only choice you have is to cooperate." And with that, she turned and followed Anthony to the car.

"They're liars," Coop repeated before Anthony even started the engine. "It's a mistake to give them an audience for whatever it is they're trying to pull."

Kade shrugged. "I have to start somewhere to get to the bottom of what happened to Bree."

"What happened to Bree is *my* concern," Coop snapped.

That was *not* the right thing to say, especially after those heated accusations that Anthony had just made. Kade had to fight once more to hang on to his temper, but Bree beat him to the punch.

"Kade and I became parents," she reminded him. And there was a bite to her voice. "What happened is most definitely his concern."

That didn't cool down the anger in Coop's face. He opened his mouth, no doubt ready to argue, but there was no argument he could give that would make Kade back off from this investigation. His baby girl's safety was at stake.

Coop gave her a look that could have frozen hell. "Be careful who you cast your lot with, Bree. It could come back to bite you."

Bree faced him head-on. "I'm always careful."

That obviously didn't please him because he cursed. "I'm giving you forty-eight hours." Coop's voice had that dangerous edge to it again. "If you're not at headquarters by then, you'll never see your badge again."

Chapter Eight

Bree watched Leah sleep and hoped the baby would wake up before Kade's brother Grayson arrived to take her to the house in San Antonio. These last minutes with her daughter were precious time, and she needed every second to count.

"Grayson will be here in about a half hour," Kade informed her when he got off the phone.

Bree had listened in on the flurry of calls that Kade had made after their guests' departures, but her main focus had been on Leah.

And her badge.

It was hard to push that aside completely, even though that's exactly what Bree wanted to do.

She'd been an agent for five years now, after she'd slogged her way through college night classes at the University of Texas and cruddy jobs so she could get her degree. And Coop had helped with that. In fact, he'd helped with a lot of things to put her on track and keep her there. He hadn't just been her boss but also her mentor and friend.

"All three of the nannies will be at the estate in San Antonio," Kade explained. "So, Leah will have lots of attention from them and her three aunts."

Still, it hurt that she wouldn't be there to share it.

"I've never thought of family as being a good thing," she mumbled. "But I'm glad Leah has yours."

"So am I." He walked back to the sofa where she was seated. "It's not too late, you know. You can go to San Antonio with them."

Mercy, that was tempting, just so she wouldn't have to leave Leah, but Bree had to shake her head. "Too big of a risk, especially since all of our suspects know I'm with you."

Bree's gaze whipped to his. "Please tell me that Grayson will take precautions when driving Leah to San Antonio. McClendon and the others can't follow him."

"They won't follow," Kade promised. "Grayson's a good lawman. And besides, his pregnant wife is at the house. He wouldn't put her or any of the rest of the family at risk."

Further risk, Bree mentally corrected. Because the risk was already there.

He sank down on the sofa next to her and touched Leah's cheek. The baby stirred a little but went straight back to sleep. Bree repeated what Kade had done and got the same results.

"Don't worry," Kade said. "You'll have time with her after this is over."

Yes, and that was another unsettled issue to go with the others. Leah. A custody arrangement. And the man next to her.

Her mind was already spinning with some possibilities. "Maybe I can move to Silver Creek. And get a regular job with the FBI." Those were things she'd considered *before* Coop's visit. "If I still have a badge, that is."

"You will," Kade promised. "Coop was just, well,

I think he was pissed that you didn't jump to go back with him. He's pretty territorial when it comes to you."

That sent her gaze back to his. "There's nothing personal between Coop and me."

"Didn't think there was on your part, but Coop's reaction could be because of guilt. He failed to protect you, and now he's trying to make sure nothing else goes wrong."

She stared at him. "Or?"

Kade shrugged. "Or Anthony's accusations could be true. We have to at least consider that Coop might be in on this. I'm having someone check his financials to see if there's a money trail that leads to the Fulbright clinic or any of our suspects."

Before today, Bree would have jumped to defend her boss. But that was before someone tried to kill her. "What about this witness that Anthony claims he has?"

Another head shake. "Anthony won't give names, but both Jamie and he are supposed to show up at the sheriff's office tomorrow. Grayson told them they'd better have proof and the witness."

That caused her stomach to churn, because she didn't want to believe that Coop could have endangered her this way. But it also gave her some relief. If Anthony maybe had proof that could lead to an arrest, then Bree wouldn't have to be away from Leah very long.

Of course, that might not end the danger.

Coop could be just a small piece in all of this. An insignificant piece. But Bree still didn't like that he could have kept a secret that would have an impact on the investigation. Not just for the Fulbright clinic but for the aftermath and what had happened to her.

"When are Anthony's and Jamie's trial dates?" she asked Kade.

"Two more weeks. I'll testify. They'll want you to do the same."

Yes, because their testimony was what would convict them of the worst of the charges since there wasn't a lot of hard evidence.

"Nothing else on those missing surveillance backups?" she pressed.

"No. We have agents looking for them, though. Agents who don't work for Coop," he added before she could voice her concern. "Even if we don't find them before the trial dates, our testimony should be enough to convict Jamie and Anthony of at least some of the charges. The security guards, too."

Because those guards had tried to kill Kade and her on that undercover assignment. Plus, she could testify about the two illegal immigrant surrogates she'd ferreted out while there. The women had said both Jamie and Anthony were responsible for them being at the clinic. Of course, the women had also since disappeared and hopefully were alive somewhere, but Bree's testimony should be sufficient.

Unless...

"McClendon's lawyers could use my ordeal to question how reliable my memories are." That didn't help with the acid in her stomach. "And we don't have proof that McClendon, Anthony or Jamie was the one who had me kidnapped."

Kade nodded and eased his arm around her. He also eased her to him. "Two weeks is a long time, Bree. Anthony's witness could pan out."

And if so, that meant Coop would be arrested or implicated in something bad. It was a long shot and one she hoped she didn't have to face.

"What if an arrest doesn't end the threat against us?" she asked.

"Then, we keep looking."

Kade pulled in a deep breath and brushed a kiss on her forehead. He didn't look at her, and it didn't seem as if he'd noticed what he had done. That made it even more scary. Had they become so comfortable with each other that a benign peck was standard?

Apparently so.

The danger was responsible for that. And Leah. Kade and she were joined at the hip now, and that wasn't likely to end anytime soon. Their situation was bringing them closer together and keeping them there. For now. But Bree knew that bubbles often burst.

"I know you're uncomfortable with all of this," Kade said. He glanced at his arm slung around her and then at the spot where he'd kissed her.

So, he had been aware of what he'd done.

"I'm comfortable," she corrected. "And that's what makes me most uncomfortable."

He laughed. It was smoky and thick. All male. And she realized it was the first time she'd heard him do that. It made her smile in spite of the mess they were in. And then the easy way she'd smiled only added to the discomfort.

Sheez.

She was in trouble here in more ways than one.

"If you take the danger out of the situation," he continued, "then what's happening between us might not be a bad thing. I mean, I'm attracted to you, and I'm pretty sure you're attracted to me. That's better than having us at each other's throats."

That created an image that she tried to push aside.

Fast. Of Kade kissing her throat. Her, kissing his. Heck, she was just fantasizing about kissing him, period.

"The attraction isn't going to make this easier," she reminded him.

He paused, made a sound of agreement. Then, made another sound that could have meant anything. "Not easier, but I can't seem to stop it. I dreamed about you."

She risked looking at him, even though that put them face-to-face with their mouths too close together. Another kiss wouldn't send them into a wild scramble to have sex on the sofa. Because Leah was there. But if the baby hadn't been, then all bets were off.

And Grayson would arrive soon to take Leah.

What then?

More dreams, no doubt.

She didn't question Kade about his dream. Didn't need to hear the details. She'd had enough hot dreams about him when they'd played under the covers at the clinic. She doubted his dreams about her could be as hot as the ones she'd had about him.

The corner of his mouth lifted, and a dimple flashed in his cheek. That smile no doubt caused many women to melt into a puddle.

And it was doing the same to her.

But the puddle cooled down when she heard the sound. It was slight. Like a little squeak. However, it was enough to send Kade and her looking down at Leah. The baby squirmed, made another of those sounds.

And her eyes finally opened.

"About time you woke up," Kade told her, and he kissed the baby on her cheek.

Bree did the same. A puddle of a different kind. How could she possibly love someone this much?

"I'll miss her," Bree whispered. And that was a huge

understatement. It would kill a piece of her to see Grayson take her baby out that door.

"Yeah," Kade agreed. It sounded as if he had a lump in his throat. He opened his mouth to say more, but another sound stopped him.

Footsteps.

And that meant Grayson had likely arrived to take Leah away. Bree instantly had to blink back tears.

However, it was Mason who appeared in the doorway, and while he wasn't exactly out of breath, he had obviously hurried. He was also carrying a laptop. "We have another problem," he told them.

Bree groaned. "Not another visitor?"

"Of sorts," Mason verified. "You guys are real popular today. Someone just scaled over the fence. And that someone is armed."

KADE CURSED AND DREW HIS GUN. He didn't want a confrontation with a gunman. Especially not with Leah still in the house. Not with Bree there, either.

Mason put the laptop on the table in front of them. The screen was split into six frames, each of them showing the feed from the various security cameras positioned around the grounds. Mason pointed to the top right where Kade could see an armed man behind a tree. He was armed all right.

A rifle with a scope.

Bree pulled Leah even closer to her. "How far away is he from the house?"

"Half mile," Mason answered.

But the moment Mason spoke, the guy darted out and raced for cover behind another tree. He was moving closer to the house. Closer to Leah.

"I've alerted the ranch hands," Mason continued. He drew his gun. "And I'm about to head out there myself."

Kade wanted to go with him. He wanted to be the one to confront this SOB and one way or another get some answers from him.

But that would mean leaving Bree and Leah alone.

He couldn't do that. Too big of a risk.

"I'll watch the surveillance and call you if there's a problem," Kade assured his brother.

Mason nodded, switched his phone to the vibrate mode so that it wouldn't be heard, and he hurried out of the room.

Bree moved closer to the laptop screen, her attention fastened on the man who was wearing dark camouflage pants and shirt. He had a black cap that obscured the upper part of his face.

"How tall do you think he is?" Bree asked.

"Six feet, maybe." He glanced at her. "Why? Do you recognize him?"

She kept studying him. "Maybe. I think it could be the man who kidnapped me. There's something about the way he's holding that rifle that looks familiar."

Then Kade wanted the man alive. Of course, his brother already knew that. Because this goon could give them answers. Kade wasn't sure if he could keep his temper in check if this was the man who'd put Bree through hell and back.

"Your captor held a rifle on you?" Kade wanted to know.

Bree nodded, and that only added to the anger he'd felt. Each little piece of information only worsened the description of hell that she'd been put through.

The gunman moved again, going behind another tree. The shift in position only highlighted more of his face. Kade couldn't see the guy's eyes, but they had a clearer image of his mouth and chin.

"Recognize him?" Kade pressed.

Bree shook her head. "I never saw his face," she reminded him. "Nor the woman's."

Still, it was obvious that she thought this could be the guy, and that was enough for Kade.

Kade looked at Leah to make sure she was okay, and thankfully she'd fallen back asleep. His baby girl didn't have a clue what was going on, but he didn't want her sensing any of Bree's fear. Except maybe it wasn't fear because Bree was staring at the man as if she wanted to rip him limb from limb.

Good.

Fear was natural, but it was determination and some luck that would get them through this.

"There aren't any more trees between that part of the pasture and the house," Kade let her know. "So, if he wants to get closer to fire that rifle, he'll have to do it out in the open."

Where Mason and the ranch hands could spot him. And hopefully stop him. But just in case the guy managed to get off a shot, Kade needed to take some more precautions.

He grabbed the laptop and took it toward the other side of the room. Toward the front of the house and far away from the windows on the rear where the gunman would no doubt be approaching. Kade helped Bree onto the floor behind the sofa. The bathtub would have been safer if it weren't for the two windows in there.

Kade kept his gun ready, and he watched. On one screen he could see Mason and three ranch hands. All armed, all headed toward the gunman. The gunman stayed put behind the tree, but he took a small device from his jacket pocket and aimed it toward the house.

"The gunman has infrared," Kade mumbled along with some profanity.

Kade fired off a text message to let Mason know that the gunman now had a way to get a visual of who was in the house. He wouldn't be able to see actual images, but he could tell from the heat blobs on his screen where they were.

"He came here to kill us." Bree's voice was barely a whisper, and Kade heard the fear now.

She turned so that her body was between Leah and the gunman. She was protecting their child, and Kade moved in front of them to do the same.

Kade braced himself for the gunman to come closer, especially now that he no doubt knew where they were.

But the man didn't do that.

He dropped the infrared device and fired. Not at the house. He fired in the direction of Mason and the ranch hands. They all dived to the ground as the bullets pelted around them.

"They're pinned down." The fear in Bree's voice went up a notch.

Kade felt his own fear rise, too, and he frantically searched the screen to see if any other ranch hands were close enough to respond and provide Mason and the others with some backup.

They weren't.

Probably because Mason had ordered everyone to stay away from possible gunfire. And they were doing just that. At least a dozen of them were guarding the house, but it wouldn't do Mason and the others any good.

"I have to go out there," Kade told Bree. He hated

to tell her this, but he had no choice. "I can approach him from this direction." He tapped the screen to the gunman's right. "While he's keeping my brother pinned down, I can sneak up on him."

Bree shook her head, but then she groaned and squeezed her eyes shut a second. She knew this had to happen.

"Be careful," she said.

"That's the plan." Kade gave Leah and her one last look. Hopefully, a reassuring one, and he grabbed the Colt .38 from the table so he could put it by Bree's side. Things would have to have gone to hell in a handbasket if she had to use it, but Kade didn't want to leave her defenseless.

He raced out of the room, barreling down the steps and out the front door. He stopped just long enough to holster his handgun and grab a rifle from the weapons' safe just off the foyer.

"Text Mason for me," Kade instructed the ranch hand guarding the front of the house. "Tell him I'm approaching the shooter from the west side."

The shots kept coming. Not rapid fire any longer, probably because the guy wanted to conserve ammunition, but the bullets were spaced out just at the right pace to keep Mason and the others on the ground.

Kade ran to the side of the house and peered around, but the angle was wrong for him to see the gunman. He headed toward the first outbuilding—the stables— and he raced along the side until he reached the back.

Now, he had the right angle.

The shooter was still a good distance away, but the guy wasn't looking in Kade's direction. Or, thankfully, the direction of the house.

Kade took aim. Not for a kill shot. But for the man's right arm.

And he fired.

The shot blasted through the air. Kade saw the man's body snap back when the bullet slammed into his shoulder.

But the shooter didn't drop the rifle.

Despite the bullet wound, the guy pivoted, lightning fast, aimed at Kade. And he fired.

Kade ducked behind the stables in the nick of time. The shot slammed into the exterior wall in the exact spot where his head had just been.

Whoever this guy was, he wasn't an amateur.

Kade stayed low, glanced around the stables, but before he could get a good look, another shot came at him.

Then another.

Kade tried to see this as a good thing. This way, Mason might be able to return fire, but it was hard to see the good side of things with the bullets coming at him.

He got even lower to the ground and looked out again. The man had taken aim but not at Kade.

At the house.

His heart went to his knees. Yes, Bree and Leah were somewhat protected, but this guy could maybe get off a lucky shot.

Kade couldn't risk that.

He came out from the stables, his rifle already aimed at the intended target. No arm shot this time. He went for the kill.

And Kade pulled the trigger.

Even from this distance, he heard the sickening thud of the bullet tearing into the shooter's body. The man's rifle dropped to the ground.

Seconds later, so did the man.

Kade started running toward him.

Maybe, just maybe, he could get to him in time, before he took his last breath. And then Kade could learn the identity of the person who'd sent this monster after Bree and his baby.

Chapter Nine

Bree almost wished the latest adrenaline crash would numb her to the fear and desperation that she was feeling. Not for herself.

But for Leah.

Their situation wasn't getting better, and judging from Kade's stark expression, he felt the same way. He sat across from her, his elbows on his knees and his face in his hands.

"I'm sorry," he repeated to her.

"You had no choice but to kill him." Bree knew that was true because she'd watched the nightmarish ordeal play out in front of her on the laptop screen.

First, she'd been terrified that Kade, his brother or one of the others would be killed. Then, her terror had skyrocketed when the shooter took aim at the house. For a couple of horrifying moments, Bree had thought he might shoot. That a bullet could tear through the walls and reach Leah.

But Kade had made sure that didn't happen. The gunman hadn't even had time to pull the trigger again before Kade shot him.

And killed him.

She'd watched that, too, while she'd held her baby close and prayed that nothing else bad would happen.

Leah was okay, thank God. But the shooter hadn't been able to say anything before Kade got to him. No dying confession to clear his conscience, and that meant they were right back at square one.

Well, almost.

Kade's brother Grayson had arrived just minutes after the fatal shooting and immediately taken over the necessary mop-up of an inevitable investigation. Grayson was pacing their suite while talking on the phone, and from what Bree could glean from the conversation, he was within minutes of turning over the investigation to one of his deputies so he could leave for San Antonio.

With Leah, of course.

That was good, Bree kept reminding herself. However, in this case *good* felt like something beyond bad.

"We're doing the right thing sending Leah with Grayson," she whispered. She tried not to make it sound like a question, but it did, anyway. She prayed she wasn't sending her baby from the frying pan into the fire.

Kade eased down his hands, looked at her. Then looked at Leah, who was in Bree's lap. "Yeah." He no doubt knew everything Bree was feeling because he was feeling it, too. He paused. "I also need to make arrangements for you."

Bree shook her head. "Once Leah is away from the danger, what I'd really like is a showdown with whoever's responsible for this."

That sent another jolt of anger through her. She wanted to find this person fast and be the one to put them in jail or do what Kade had just done. End it with a bullet.

"You're up for that?" Kade questioned.

Probably not. Her hands were still shaky, and she felt years removed from her FBI training. Right now, she felt like a mother with a child who'd just been placed in harm's way. And that was a far stronger motivation than she'd ever had to bring down a criminal.

Bree touched her daughter's cheek, and even though Leah's eyes were closed, she gave Bree one of those baby smiles. The feeling of warmth replaced the anger. But not the determination for Bree to keep her safe.

However, Leah wasn't the only person for her to be concerned about.

"Are you okay?" she asked Kade. "And before you give me a blanket *I'm fine* answer, I'd like the truth."

Kade stayed quiet a moment. "Ever killed a man in the line of duty?"

"Once." A cut-and-dried case of defending herself, just as Kade had done.

"It doesn't get easier," Kade mumbled.

Bree rubbed his arm and hoped that would help. But how could it? He'd done what he had to do, but he'd also have to come to terms with taking a life.

Yet something else they had in common.

As if they needed more.

Sometimes, like now, Bree felt that Kade and she were speeding headfirst, no helmets, into a brick wall. One of them, or both, would get hurt, but there didn't seem to be anything that would stop it. She didn't know whether to fight it or just save her energy and surrender.

Grayson ended his call, and when he didn't make another one, both Kade and Bree looked at him.

"The dead shooter's name is Tim Kirk," Grayson explained. "He worked as a security guard at the Fulbright clinic during your undercover investigation."

Maybe that's why he'd seemed familiar to Bree. "Kirk's connected to one of our suspects?" And she didn't include Coop in that list, despite what Anthony had told them during his visit to the ranch.

"He is. And he's also connected to the man who tried to kill you at the motel. Mason checked Kirk's cell, and yesterday morning he called the prepaid phone of the triggerman who turned up dead." Grayson paused. "However, the last person he called was Anthony."

Anthony, who'd accused Coop of wrongdoing. Of course, that accusation hadn't gotten Anthony's name off their suspect list. Now he was at the top of it.

"SAPD is sending someone over to Tim Kirk's apartment to check it out now. There might be more evidence linking him to Anthony. Or one of the others," Grayson added.

Maybe Coop, judging from Grayson's tone. Well, good. Bree wanted them to look, but she was sure they wouldn't find anything.

"While they're at Kirk's place, I hope they'll search for those surveillance backups that went missing from the Fulbright clinic," Kade reminded him.

"They will." Grayson shrugged. "But unless Kirk was planning to use them to pin the blame on someone else, those backups might have been destroyed."

Yes, Bree had considered that. She had also considered if that had happened, they might never have enough evidence to convict any of their suspects to long jail sentences. Heck, it was possible that even with a conviction Anthony and Jamie would get as little as probation.

Kade and she needed more evidence.

Grayson looked at Bree. "Any luck remembering where you were held during your pregnancy? Because there might still be some evidence there we can use."

Bree pushed her hair from her face and forced herself to think. "It was a house in the country." Which she'd already told them. "High brick fence with guard dogs. Dobermans." She shook her head. "I can remember the rooms clearly now, but I can't tell you what was past that fence."

If that disappointed Grayson, he didn't show it. "When one of the kidnappers helped you escape, do you have any idea how long it took you to get from the fenced house to the motel?"

Those images weren't so clear. In fact, they were nonexistent.

"I don't have a clue about the time frame, but I do know we didn't go directly from the house to the Treetop motel. We went to another hotel first. In Austin, I think. And she gave me a heavy dose of drugs before we left." Bree stopped a moment. "But she was in a hurry. The man wasn't there, and she said we had to get out before he came back because he was going to kill me."

Since Kade's leg was touching her, she felt him tense. "Why did he want to kill you?" Kade asked. "Leah was gone by then. Why did he or his boss feel you were no longer of any use to them?"

Again, Bree forced herself to think. "Maybe I saw something. Or maybe something changed in his situation. His boss might have found a different kind of leverage to tamper with the investigation."

But what?

Bree drew a blank on all counts.

"It sounds as if you were around the female kidnapper a lot," Grayson commented. "Any chance it was Jamie Greer?"

"A good chance," Bree admitted. "The height and body build are a match." Still, she had to shake her head. "But she certainly didn't dress like Jamie, and the prosthetic mask was very good. I couldn't see any of her features behind it." She shrugged. "Of course, the drugs probably helped with that. Hard to see a person's features when they're swimming in and out of focus."

"Keep trying to remember," Grayson insisted after a nod. He checked the time and blew out a weary breath. "McClendon, Anthony and Jamie are all on their way to my office. Or they sure as heck better be. If not, I warned them they'd all be arrested."

Good. Maybe they would defy that order, and that would get them tossed in jail. A temporary stay was better than nothing.

"I need you to help Mason question them," Grayson added, his attention on Kade. "Are you up to it?"

"Absolutely." Kade got to his feet. "Anthony accused Bree's boss of being a dirty agent, said he had a witness. Maybe he'll bring that witness with him."

Bree adjusted the baby to the crook of her arm and stood, too. "I'd like to get in on this."

The brothers exchanged glances and were no doubt thinking she wasn't mentally or physically ready for this. She wasn't, but that wouldn't stop her. "When I hear what they have to say, it might help me remember where I was held captive."

Grayson finally nodded. "Tape the interviews and follow the rules. If one of them is guilty, I don't want them slipping through the cracks on a technicality."

Bree was on the same page with that. Someone would pay for what had happened. Hopefully, it wouldn't be Kade, her or Leah.

"It's time," Grayson said, and with those two little words, Bree knew exactly what he meant.

Kade did, as well, because he leaned over and kissed

Leah's cheek. "This won't be for long," he promised the baby in a whisper.

Bree kissed her, as well, but she didn't trust her voice to speak. Oh, mercy. This was much harder than she'd imagined it would be; something she hadn't thought possible.

"Three of the ranch hands are making the drive with us," Grayson let them know. He picked up the diaper bag, looped it over his shoulder and then walked closer.

Waiting for Bree to hand Leah over.

Bree gave her baby one last kiss. Kade did the same. And she eased Leah into Grayson's waiting arms.

"I'll take good care of her," Grayson promised. And just like that, he hurried out of the room.

Bree's heart went with him.

Tears stung her eyes, and she blinked them back when Kade slipped his arm around her.

"Everything will be okay," he said, his voice clogged with emotion. He cleared his throat. "And the sooner we question our suspects, the sooner we can maybe end this."

So that Leah could come home.

Well, come to the ranch, anyway. It was her home, of course, but Bree knew that might change when Kade and she worked out some sort of custody arrangement.

"Let's go to the sheriff's office," he insisted, and with his arm still around her, he led her to the door where Grayson had just exited.

Kade stopped.

He looked down at her and opened his mouth. Closed it. Then shook his head. "Later," he mumbled.

Bree nearly pressed him for an answer, but she wasn't sure she wanted to open any cans of worms with Kade right now. One thing at a time, and the first thing was to get through these interrogations.

By the time they made it outside to Kade's truck, Grayson had already driven away. *To safety,* Bree reminded herself again. And if Kade and she could do their jobs and make an arrest, their time apart from Leah would be minimized. That was all the motivation she needed to end this quickly.

"What if Anthony produces a witness who says that Coop is dirty?" Kade asked her. He started his truck and headed for town.

"Then, I'll assume Anthony paid off the person to lie." Bree figured this wasn't the answer Kade wanted to hear. She stared at him. "Why are you so willing to believe Coop worked for McClendon?"

He stayed quiet a moment, mumbled something she didn't quite catch. "For the worst of reasons." Another pause. "I think I might be jealous of him."

"What?" Bree couldn't get that out there fast enough.

"This is hard for me to admit, but Coop seems possessive of you."

"In a boss to employee sort of way," she clarified. "There has never been anything personal between Coop and me."

"You're sure he knows that?"

Again, she jumped to answer, but then stopped. And Bree remembered something that'd happened over a year ago. "Coop kissed me."

"He did what?" Kade volleyed glances between the road and her.

"He'd had too much to drink. And he apologized."

Kade made a *yeah-right* sound.

"Hey, you kissed me, and you apologized," Bree reminded him.

"The apology was a lie. I'm attracted to you and so is Coop." He cursed. "But that attraction probably means he wouldn't betray you."

Bree felt relieved. For a moment. However, the uneasy feeling came. "I pushed him away that night," she recalled. "I told him I didn't feel that way about him."

She waited for Kade to say something about a scorned man seeking revenge, but he only shrugged. "If you hadn't been kidnapped, he probably would have tried again. I would have," Kade added in a mumble.

Bree stared at him. Yes, he would have. "If you hadn't, I would have," she confessed. "And if you think that pleases me, think again."

Despite the seriousness of the conversation, the corner of his mouth lifted, and she got a hint of that killer smile once more. "I just don't want you to think that the attraction I feel for you has anything to do with Leah."

She'd been on the verge of smiling herself, but that stopped it. Bree shook her head.

"I'm not trying to work out custody issues with you in bed," he clarified.

Oh.

At first there was a jolt of anger, that maybe Kade would think that's what she was trying to do. But she kept staring at him and didn't see any sign of it.

The only sign she saw was the confirmation that what she felt for him had zilch to do with Leah. Or with the danger. It had to do with the fact that he was, well, hot.

She groaned and leaned her head against the window. "Sex should be the last thing on my mind right now."

"Yeah," Kade agreed.

That didn't make it true.

Both of them knew that.

"I'm thinking when you're a hundred percent, we just get it over," he continued. "I mean, we worked ourselves up on the assignment. Now the close contact is steaming things up again. If we could just find the time to jump into bed, that might cool us down."

Her smile came, anyway. "Is that some kind of invitation to your bed?" Oh, yes. Headfirst into that brick wall.

He took her hand, lifted it and brought it to his mouth to kiss. "I already have you in my bed, but you're not in any shape for sex."

Her mind agreed.

Her body didn't.

And Bree was about to blurt that out when Kade's phone buzzed. He answered it but said little so she couldn't tell if the caller was Grayson. Soon, she'd want to contact Kade's brother and make sure the trip to San Antonio had gone smoothly.

Bree prayed it had.

"Let me know if you find anything," Kade said to the caller, and he hung up. "That was Nate, my brother at SAPD. It's not about Leah," he quickly added.

Good thing, too. Her mind wasn't going in a good direction on this.

"Nate sent one of his detectives to Tim Kirk's apartment, but it's been ransacked. His wall safe had been opened, and it was empty."

Definitely not good. Any potential evidence had probably been destroyed or contaminated. Still, Bree had a gut feeling that Kirk was the person who'd kidnapped her. Proving it, though, would be a bear.

But then, as Kade was pulling into the parking lot of the sheriff's office, she saw someone who could maybe clear all of this up.

Anthony.

He was heading inside the front door of the building. For the interview no doubt, but he clearly wasn't happy about being there. And he was alone.

No witness.

However, that wasn't the only thing Bree wanted to question Anthony about. It was that phone call that Kirk had made to him.

Kade and she got out of the truck, and both checked their surroundings. Old habits. Plus, the events of the morning still had her on edge. Bree wished that she'd at least brought a firearm with her just in case someone had already hired another hit man, but she'd given Kade back the little Colt that he carried in his ankle holster.

They stepped inside the back entrance, but the sound of the voice stopped them. A voice that Bree recognized.

Hector McClendon.

And whomever he was talking to, it wasn't a friendly conversation. McClendon was speaking in whispers, but the anger in his tone came through loud and clear.

Kade pointed to the last room on the right and put his finger to his mouth in a stay-quiet gesture. Bree did, and she listened.

"I don't know what game you're trying to play," McClendon snarled. "But I'm warning you to keep your mouth shut. If you don't, Bree Winston isn't the only person who'll be on the business end of a rifle."

Chapter Ten

Kade couldn't wait to see the face of the person that Hector McClendon had just threatened. He stepped into the doorway.

And saw Jamie Greer.

Both McClendon and Jamie snapped toward Kade and Bree. Jamie's eyes were wide, and she appeared to be shaken. Not McClendon, though. He just cursed. It was ripe, raw and aimed at Kade and Bree.

Especially Bree.

The venomous look the man gave her made Kade want to punch his lights out. *Great.* No objectivity left, and while punching McClendon might make him feel a little better, it wouldn't do anything to help their investigation.

"Eavesdropping," McClendon barked. "Figures."

Kade shrugged. "If you want your death threats to be more private, maybe you shouldn't do them in a sheriff's office."

"It wasn't a death threat. It was a warning."

"Sounded like a death threat to me," Bree spoke up.

Kade waited, gauging Jamie's reaction, but the woman didn't have much of one other than the obvious fear.

"Deputy Garza is waiting to interview me," Jamie

said, and she stepped around the three of them and headed up the hall.

Deputy Melissa Garza, known as Mel, would no doubt fill in Kade later if Jamie volunteered more about the threat.

"And your brother is waiting to interview me," McClendon informed them.

Bree blocked the man's path when he started out of the room. "Just to let you know, your intimidation tactics won't work. I'm testifying against Anthony and Jamie, and I'll testify against you too the second charges are filed. And they will be filed."

"Really?" McClendon stayed calm and cool. "You'd testify against me? You think a jury will listen to a woman who has gaps the size of Texas in her memory?"

Bree looked ready to demand how he knew about her memory issues, but she stepped back. The man was on a fishing expedition, probably, and Kade didn't want Bree to provide him with anything that he could in turn feed to his team of attorneys.

Well, McClendon couldn't have known about the memory gaps unless Coop had told him. But Kade had enough on his plate without looking for another angle on this. And the biggest thing on his plate came walking up the hall toward him.

Hector McClendon's son, Anthony.

He spared his father a glance. The two didn't speak. The senior McClendon walked off and disappeared into one of the interview rooms where his attorneys and Mason were no doubt waiting for him.

"I told you that Coop would try to silence you," Anthony said to Bree the moment they were alone.

Kade didn't respond, but he did step into the interview room across the hall, and he motioned for Anthony and Bree to join him. Once they were inside, Kade made a show of hitting the record button on the camera that was mounted in the corner.

Anthony's eyes narrowed, first at the camera, then at Bree.

"I stand by what I said," Anthony insisted. He sank down into one of the chairs.

Bree leaned against the wall. "But yet you didn't bring the witness who could corroborate your allegation."

His eyes narrowed even more. "The witness wasn't available at such short notice. Tomorrow."

Kade wouldn't hold his breath. He took the chair across the table from Anthony, whirled it around and sat with the chair back facing Anthony.

"Today, we'll talk about Tim Kirk," Kade started. "Oh, and for the record, you do know you have the right to remain silent and the right to have an attorney present—"

"You're reading me my rights? Well, I already know them." He paused only to draw breath. "You planning to take me back in into custody, Agent Ryland? Because I have to tell you that I'll press to have your badge removed for an illegal detainment."

"Won't be illegal if I have cause," Kade tossed back.

"Tim Kirk," Bree prompted. She moved closer, propped her hip on the edge of the table and put on her best law enforcement face. "He tried to kill us earlier."

Anthony couldn't have looked more disinterested. "So?"

"So, guess who was the last person Kirk called before the attempted murder of two federal agents, a deputy sheriff, multiple civilians and a seven-week-old baby?"

Now Anthony was interested, and those once-narrowed eyes widened. "He didn't call me."

Kade nodded. "Yeah. He did. And unlike your mystery witness, I have real proof of it. I have Kirk's cell phone."

"Well, I don't have mine. It went missing yesterday." Anthony stopped and groaned. "I thought I'd lost it, but it's obvious someone stole it so they could set me up."

Kade huffed. Of course the man would come up with something. "Who would do that to you?" Kade pressed. And he would bet his next paycheck that Coop's name was going to roll off Anthony's tongue.

But it's a bet he would have lost.

"My father," Anthony answered.

Bree flexed her eyebrows. "And why would he do that?"

"To make me look guilty, of course. Don't you see? He's desperate, especially since his overpriced lawyers haven't been able to stop the investigation. Now that you're back in the picture, he's got to be thinking he's just days away from being arrested on something more serious than misdemeanors."

Bree and Kade exchanged glances, and she was probably thinking about the encounter they'd just overheard between McClendon and Jamie. Anthony was right about one thing—his father was indeed desperate.

"You have any proof that your father stole your phone?" Kade asked.

Anthony shook his head. "But he had the opportunity because he came to see me last night. He could have taken it when I stepped out of the room to take a call on my house phone."

Bree stared at the man, probably trying to determine if everything coming out of his mouth was a pack of lies.

Or the truth that made his father look very guilty.

"Why did he visit you?" Bree questioned.

"Probably to steal my phone," Anthony practically yelled, but he settled down almost immediately. "He said he was worried about you, that the person who kidnapped you probably wasn't done. That he or she would want you dead because you might remember something that would get the person arrested."

"Persons," Bree corrected. "Two people held me captive, and I think one of them was Tim Kirk. He's linked to you with that phone call."

"Keep digging. He's linked to my father, too, because dear ol' dad is the one who hired Kirk to work at the clinic. Security," he added with a smirk. "The man was as dirty as they came, and my father hired him."

That may be, but it still didn't mean McClendon had paid Kirk to kidnap Bree or to try to kill her.

"Go ahead, access my cell phone records," Anthony insisted. "Maybe you'll be able to see that the phone wasn't at my house. I tell you, my father stole it."

Kade wasn't sure he could get that kind of info from the records, but he'd try. After all, he was pretty sure McClendon was a criminal for the things that had gone on at the clinic, and it wasn't much of a stretch for the man to try to put the blame on someone else.

Including his own son.

Anthony stood. "I think I should consult my lawyer now. Because it's clear I'm not making any headway with you two. Believe what you will. But watch your backs when you're around my father or any of his cronies. That includes Agent Cooper."

Kade considered stopping Anthony. Maybe putting

him in lockup for a few hours until his lawyer could arrive. But that wouldn't accomplish much other than to give Kade some satisfaction that someone was paying for what'd happened to Bree. The problem was, he wasn't sure Anthony was the right someone.

So he let the man walk.

Kade stood, turned off the camera just as Bree huffed.

"How soon can you get someone on Anthony's cell records?" she asked.

"I can do that with a phone call." Kade paused. "And while I'm doing that, I can see what's happening with the search into Coop's financials."

That hit a nerve. Bree dodged his gaze, huffed again. "I'm guessing the agents have found nothing or they would have called."

"Yeah, that's my guess, too." Another pause. "That doesn't mean they won't find something eventually."

"I know." She nodded. "I know. But unless they do, McClendon and Anthony are looking better and better for this. Is there a chance we can get Anthony's bond revoked, or bring some charges, any charges, against McClendon?"

"It's possible." And Kade would try. "There were some financial irregularities at the clinic that we could use to arrest McClendon. But either of them could still try to get to you even if they're behind bars."

He ran his hand down the length of her arm. Felt her shudder. She was no doubt reliving the worst of the moments of the attacks that had led up to this.

"Let's go back to the ranch. Mason and the other deputies can handle these interviews, and I'll see about setting up a video call with Grayson."

Her eyes lit up. "So we can see Leah."

Yeah. Seeing images of their baby would have to do for now. And maybe it wouldn't be long before they had the real thing.

Kade led her into the hall, but they'd made it just a few steps before Jamie stepped into the hall, as well.

"I have to speak to you," she mouthed. And she looked all around as if she expected them to be ambushed.

That put Kade on full alert, and he eased Bree behind him. He put his hand on the gun in his holster.

"What do you want?" Kade asked, and he didn't use his polite voice. He was sick and tired of all the suspects and just wanted to get Bree out of there.

Jamie looked over her shoulder again and reached into her purse. That had Kade tightening the grip on his gun, but Jamie didn't draw a firearm. She pulled out a small folded piece of paper and handed it to Bree.

"Read it," Jamie instructed. "Not here. And don't let anyone else know that I gave it to you. If anyone else is involved, I'll call the whole thing off."

Kade had no idea what Jamie was talking about. Apparently neither did Bree because she started to unfold the note.

"Not here," Jamie repeated, her voice still barely above a whisper. "It's not safe for anyone else to know."

And with that cryptic warning hanging in the air, Jamie turned and walked back into the interview room.

BREE LOOKED AT JAMIE'S note again, even though she already knew what it said. The message was simple:

I'll call you to arrange a meeting for tomorrow. By then, I'll have the answers you need.

"Answers," Bree mumbled.

Well, Kade and she were certainly short of those, but she wasn't sure that Jamie would be the one to provide them.

Neither was Kade.

"It could be a trap," Kade said, glancing at the note while he drove them back to the ranch.

Yes, it could be. Plus, there was another question. "Why didn't Jamie just give us these *answers* while we were at the sheriff's office?"

Kade lifted his shoulder. "Maybe because McClendon was there. Or maybe she doesn't have them *yet.*"

Well, McClendon had threatened her just minutes earlier, so Jamie could be afraid of him. Still, something didn't add up. Bree wanted to suggest that they go back to the office and demand information, but that might cause Jamie to take back her offer.

Right now, that offer was pretty much all they had.

"So, what? We just wait for Jamie's call?" she asked.

He nodded though he didn't seem very eager to walk into a trap. Of course, doing nothing was just as dangerous. Bree was willing to do whatever it took to speed up the investigation and get Leah back.

Kade parked his truck directly in front of the ranch house porch, and even though there were several ranch hands there for their protection, Kade didn't dawdle. He held on to Bree and practically raced inside. Once he had the door shut, he armed the security system.

Bree stood there a moment to catch her breath and try to absorb everything that'd happened. Kade must have needed the same thing because he leaned against the door and drew in a long breath. But the breath-taking moment was over quickly.

"Our cook is at the estate in San Antonio, but I'll fix you some lunch," he said.

However, Kade had barely made it a step when his phone rang.

Kade mumbled something and pushed the button to answer the call on speaker.

"You're having me investigated," Coop immediately said. "You had someone dig into my financials."

"I did," Kade readily admitted. "It's standard procedure. Anthony McClendon made an accusation about you providing security to the clinic, and I had to check it out. Just as I've done with all leads."

"It's a witch hunt, and you know it." Coop's voice was so strained with anger that Bree barely recognized it.

She thought of the conversation earlier when Kade had admitted that he might be jealous of Coop. Bree was still trying to wrap her mind around that, but she didn't think for one second that jealousy was what had motivated Kade to investigate Coop.

"This had to be done, Coop," Bree spoke up. "We had to rule you out as a suspect. Standard procedure. You would have done the same thing if you were in my place."

Silence.

Her heart skipped a beat. "The investigation will rule you out, right?" And Bree hated that it was a question.

More silence, followed by more profanity. "It'll only muddy the waters more than they already are."

When Coop didn't add more, Bree glanced at Kade. And then she tried to brace herself for whatever they were about to hear from a man she'd been positive she could trust.

"I take security jobs on the side," Coop finally said.

"It helps with the child support and my old college loans."

Oh, mercy. "Did you work for McClendon at the Fulbright clinic?" Bree demanded.

"Not in the way you think," Coop snapped. But he paused again. "A friend of a friend put me in contact with McClendon about eighteen months ago. McClendon said he thought hc had some employees skimming profits, and he wanted me to set up a secret security system in addition to the basic one they already had. So I did."

Each word was like a slap to the face, and Bree reached for the wall to steady her suddenly weak legs.

"Give me details," Kade ordered.

"McClendon paid me ten grand to set up equipment in his son's and Jamie Greer's offices. I monitored the surveillance for a couple of months, and then he said my services were no longer needed. That happened weeks *before* the two of you were sent in there undercover."

That wasn't exactly comforting, but it was something.

If it was true.

Bree just didn't know anymore.

"Why didn't you tell anyone this before now?" Bree asked, and she held her breath.

"Because I knew it would look bad. And I also knew it didn't have anything to do with the case. Like I said, this just muddies the waters. The whole time I was monitoring those phone taps and hidden cameras, I didn't see anything illegal going on."

Kade groaned softly and shook his head. "Are you telling me that during all of this, you didn't hear anything about the FBI's investigation of that clinic?"

"Not a word," Coop insisted.

That was possible because the investigation had been kept close to the vest, but Coop still should have come forward when he finally had heard about it.

And that brought Bree to another question that she didn't want to ask. But she had to.

"When did you learn about Kade's and my under-cover operation?"

Another stretch of silence. "Three days into it," Coop answered.

Her legs got even shakier. "The day our cover was blown and someone tried to kill us."

"I had nothing to do with that!" Coop snapped. "And I want all of this talk and accusations to go away. I've told my boss all about it, and it's the end of it. *Period.*"

Maybe the official end as far as the FBI was concerned, but it gave Bree some major doubts. Still, she couldn't believe that Coop would have known about her kidnapping and not tried to do something to stop it.

"Are you satisfied, Ryland?" The anger in Coop's voice went up a notch.

"No," Kade readily answered. "Not even close. If I find out you did something to endanger Bree and our daughter—"

"I didn't," Coop interrupted. "And everyone at the Bureau believes me. They know I'm a good agent." He paused again. "Bree, I need to see you. We need to talk alone. Say the word, and I'll drive out to see you right now."

Yes, they did need to talk, but it couldn't happen *right now.* "I'll call you when I can," she let him know.

Bree gave Kade a nod, and he pressed the end call button. They both stood there, silent, while Bree tried to absorb what she'd just learned. But that wasn't possible.

"Coop's the reason I have a badge," she managed to say.

Kade just nodded and pulled her into his arms. Until he did that, Bree hadn't known just how much she needed to be held.

This hurt, bad.

"Just wait until all the evidence is in, and we'll see where this goes," Kade said, and he pressed a kiss on her forehead. "It might not even lead back to Coop."

She eased back, looked up at him. "Even if Coop isn't dirty, he still should have said something about having worked for McClendon."

Kade could only make a sound of agreement.

And Bree felt as if her world had fallen apart.

The soft sobbing sound left her mouth before she could stop it, and it caused Kade to pull her back into his arms.

"Shhh," he whispered, his breath brushing over her face. "It'll be okay."

Bree wasn't sure she believed that and looked up to tell him, but everything seemed to stop. Not the pain. That was still there. So was the ache at being separated from Leah. But the whirlwind of thoughts about Coop and the investigation came to a grinding halt. She was instantly aware of Kade. Of his arms. Of the way he made her feel.

Without thinking, she came up on her toes and kissed Kade.

He made a sound, too. A low rumble that came from deep within his throat, and he snapped her to him until her body was pressed against his.

And he kissed her right back.

But he did more than that. Oh, yeah. More. Kade

took control of things. His mouth moved over hers, and he parted the seam of her lips with his tongue.

The taste of him roared through every inch of her. She'd known the attraction was there. Had felt it. But this was more. It was a burning fire that the kiss fanned until it seemed more like a need.

His fingers dived into her hair, anchoring her head so that he controlled the movement. He didn't stop there. He turned her and put her back against the wall. And he put himself against her.

The sensations hit her hard. Not just the heat and the need, but the feel of his body on hers. It didn't help when he took that kiss to her neck.

Bree fought to get in a different position so that she could feel more of him, and she got it finally. The alignment brought his sex against her, and the intimate contact along with his lips and tongue on her neck were making her insane. She was within seconds of dragging him to the floor so they could do this the right way.

Or the wrong way.

She caught his chin and lifted it, forcing eye contact. "Are we ready for this?" she asked.

It no doubt sounded like a joke, but there was nothing humorous in Kade's eyes. That icy gray had turned fiery hot, and it was clear that he wanted her as much as she wanted him.

"Ready?" he repeated as if it were painful just to ask the question. He dropped back an inch.

"Sex will complicate things," she settled for saying.

He thought about that a few seconds. "Yeah." And he put another inch of space between them.

Bree hated the loss of his touch and the heat, but she was also aware that both could return in a snap. What she felt for Kade wasn't just going to disappear.

"When we have sex," he said, "it probably shouldn't happen on the foyer floor."

For some reason that made her smile. "The place is optional," she let him know. "But the timing isn't."

Almost reluctantly, he nodded. "Soon, then." And he came back at her with a kiss that could melt metal.

He pulled away, leaving her breathless and making her rethink her decision to delay this, just as Kade's phone buzzed again. She groaned because she thought it might be Coop, but this time it was Jamie.

As he'd done with Coop's call, Kade took the call on speaker. "We read your note," Kade greeted. "You have answers? Well, I'd like to hear them *now*."

"Not yet," Jamie answered, her voice strained with fear.

Or something.

Bree wasn't about to take anything this woman said at face value.

"Meet me tomorrow morning, both of you," Jamie explained. "Nine a.m. at the pond that's in the park on the edge of town. If you bring anyone else with you, the meeting is off. You'll never learn the truth."

Bree got a very uneasy feeling about this.

Apparently, so did Kade. "What truth?" he demanded.

Jamie groaned softly. "The truth about what *really* happened to Bree after she was kidnapped."

Chapter Eleven

Kade wasn't at all sure this meeting should happen, and Jamie's one condition had made him even more concerned.

They were supposed to come alone, or the meeting was off.

Kade understood Jamie's fear—feigned or otherwise—but he had a greater need to keep Bree safe. That's why he was taking precautions without violating Jamie's *come alone* command.

He ended the call with Mason and glanced over at Bree on the passenger's seat beside him. Her attention was fastened to the rearview mirror, no doubt making sure no one was following them. She also had her hand on the gun in the shoulder holster that he'd lent her.

After all, they could be driving into a trap, and he hadn't wanted her unarmed. Since he couldn't tuck her away safely, the next best thing was to use her agent's training to get them out of this.

"Mason's in place at the park," Kade relayed to her. "He's across from the pond and hidden in some trees. Jamie arrived a few minutes ago."

"Good." She paused. "Was Mason able to secure the area before Jamie got there?"

"More or less." It was the *less* part that was giving

Kade some second and third thoughts about this, and it wasn't too late to turn his truck around and head back to the ranch.

But then, they wouldn't be any closer to ending this investigation.

"Mason is armed with a rifle in case something goes wrong, and he has one of the ranch hands with him," Kade explained. "But there are a lot of places to hide in that park. Jamie could already have someone in place."

And by someone, he meant another hit man.

"You could wait at the sheriff's office," he suggested. After looking at her, he didn't want her in danger. So much for relying on her training. "I'll call Jamie and renegotiate another meeting place. A safer one."

"She'll just say no, and one restless night away from Leah has been enough. I want this to end."

Yeah. He couldn't disagree with that. Being away from Leah had sucked, but this meeting and Bree had also contributed to his lack of sleep.

Kade blamed himself for the Bree part.

The kissing session had left his body burning for her, and even though she'd slept in the guest room just up the hall from him, that brainless part of him below the waist hadn't let him forget that Bree was nearby. Brainless had also reminded him repeatedly that if he pushed, he could have Bree in his bed.

But it was wrong to push.

Even if he wanted to badly.

No, this was one of those situations where he had to leave the decision making to his brain.

Kade kept driving, through town and past the sheriff's office. Deputy Melissa Garza was inside and monitoring the lone security camera at the park. It wasn't at the best angle, but if she saw someone approaching the pond area, she had instructions to call Mason.

Not a foolproof plan, but maybe they'd get lucky.

He took the turn into the park and was thankful to see it practically deserted. Probably because it was a weekday, and it was still a little too early for an outing. Kade drove to the pond that was on the back side of the twenty-acre area, and he parked as close to it as he could. He had no trouble spotting Jamie.

The woman was seated at a picnic table and was wearing a dark green pants outfit that blended in with the summer grass and the leafy trees. She had on her usual sunshades and a baseball cap—probably her attempt at a disguise. Hard to disguise that bright auburn hair. She stood the moment Kade and Bree stepped from his truck.

"You came," she said on a rise of breath. Her skeptical tone let Kade know that she hadn't expected him to follow through.

Or else she was acting.

"You didn't give us much choice," Bree informed her. Like Kade, she kept watch on their surroundings. And on Jamie. Bree kept studying the woman to make sure she didn't draw a weapon on them.

"Let's make this quick," Kade told her right off the bat. "Give us the *answers* so we can get the hell out of here."

Jamie nodded, swallowed hard. "I want to make a deal. Immunity from prosecution in exchange for information."

Interesting. But somewhat predictable. Jamie was facing some jail time. "What information?"

But Jamie shook her head. "I need your word that you'll help me work a deal with the D.A."

Kade didn't jump to answer but finally said, "Sure." It was a lie. Maybe. If Jamie did help them end this, then he would see what he could do.

Jamie didn't jump to answer, either, and she sank back down on the table's bench. "About ten months ago I got a call from Tim Kirk, and he said there was a security problem that had to do with something going on at the clinic. He gave me an address to a house in the Hill Country, and when I got there, he was holding Bree captive. She'd been heavily drugged."

Bree pulled in a quick breath, and Kade figured she'd be taking a lot of those in the next few minutes.

"Why didn't you call the police or the FBI?" Bree asked.

Jamie glanced around again. "Because Kirk was blackmailing me. I signed off on one of the questionable surrogate deals."

"You mean an illegal deal," Kade corrected.

"Yes," Jamie said, her mouth tight now. "I didn't want to go to jail, and I thought he was only going to hold Bree long enough to try to influence the investigation."

"Influence?" Bree repeated. She cursed. "You let him inseminate me."

"I also helped you!" But the burst of energy seemed to drain her, and Jamie groaned. She turned that shaded gaze in Kade's direction. "I don't know who was paying Kirk, but the plan was to force you to destroy all the evidence that could incriminate anyone. Including me."

Ah, he got it now. "That's why you went along with it." So that there would be no evidence against her. But there was a problem. "The FBI doesn't have all the possible evidence so there's no way Bree or I could have destroyed it all. There are missing surveillance backups."

Jamie shook her head. "I have the backups."

Kade didn't know who looked more shocked—Bree or him. Now, this was something he hadn't expected to hear in the meeting.

"Where are they?" he demanded.

"Hidden safely away. They're my insurance that Kirk's boss won't come after me. He knows there's enough incriminating evidence on them to put him in jail for years. McClendon knows I have them, too."

Well, that explained the threat McClendon had made at the sheriff's office.

"McClendon knows you're trying to cut a deal with us?" Bree asked her.

"I don't think so." But Jamie didn't sound at all convinced of that. "McClendon threatens me a lot, but I've told him that if something happens to me, then those backups will find their way to the FBI."

Kade gave that some thought. If what Jamie was saying was true, this gave McClendon motive for trying to use Bree. Of course, maybe those backups showed someone else engaged in criminal activity.

Like Coop.

Anthony.

Or even Jamie herself.

"You can give us a copy of the backups," Kade suggested. "And that way you'd still have the originals to keep yourself safe."

"The backups can't be copied," Jamie explained. "It's the way McClendon set up the system. The backups have an embedded code to wipe them clean if anyone tries to burn a copy."

Well, hell. Now Kade had to figure out a way to get the originals from Jamie. If the woman really had them, that is.

He wasn't sure she was telling the truth. About this. Or about anything else.

"I wasn't there when Kirk or whomever did the insemination on Bree," Jamie went on. "I wasn't there for the C-section, either. But later Kirk told me that the obstetrician had been killed." Jamie shivered. "He even showed me a picture of a mutilated body and said the same thing would happen to me if I didn't keep my mouth shut."

Kade huffed. "You're an accessory to murder."

Jamie frantically shook her head. "No. I swear, I didn't know until afterward, and that's when I knew I had to do something. Kirk was saying they didn't need Bree anymore, that the baby was leverage enough to get you to cooperate."

Yes, and it might have worked. Kade would have done anything to protect Leah.

"So, how did you talk Kirk into keeping me instead of Leah?" Bree asked.

"I didn't. Couldn't," Jamie corrected. "He ordered me to take the baby to a house in San Antonio where a nanny was waiting and when I returned he was going to kill you. Instead, I drove the baby to the Silver Creek hospital and left her there."

Because Bree didn't look too steady on her feet, Kade moved closer to her. Not too close, though, because he wanted them both to have room to draw their guns if something went wrong. There was still a chance of that happening. Whoever had hired Kirk wouldn't want Jamie to spill this.

"Kirk couldn't have been pleased about you not delivering the baby to San Antonio." Kade made a circling motion for Jamie to continue.

Jamie touched her hand to her lips. Her fingers and

mouth were trembling. "He wasn't. I told him someone had run me off the road and kidnapped her. He was furious and said he had to see his boss immediately. I knew I had to get Bree out of there, too."

"But you didn't, not right away," Bree reminded her. "Why?"

"Because Kirk kept watching me. He didn't trust me after what happened with the baby. Then one night I slipped him a drug, and that's when I went on the run with you. When I was sure I wasn't being followed, I left you at that motel and then made the anonymous call so Kade could come and get you. Before Kirk did."

Well, it had worked. So far. Bree and Leah were both alive, and the man partly responsible for what had happened—Kirk—was now dead.

Kade moved closer to Jamie, hoping it would make her nervous enough to tell them whatever else she was keeping from them. "Who was Kirk's boss?"

"I don't know." She answered without hesitation. "Kirk used to call him, but I never heard him say the person's name. I always assumed it was McClendon."

Good assumption.

But it could be a bad one.

Kade glanced at Bree and realized she was no doubt thinking the same thing.

Bree cleared her throat. "Did Kirk do anything else to me?"

Jamie looked in her direction for a moment. "No. Nothing like rape or torture. He just kept you drugged as much as he could. More so after the C-section."

Kade was relieved that other horrible things hadn't been done to Bree, but Jamie was wrong about the torture. Being held captive while pregnant was the stuff of nightmares, and he figured those nightmares would be with Bree for the rest of her life.

And someone would pay for that.

Kade took out the small notepad he kept in his pocket and dropped it on the table by Jamie. "Write down the address of the house where Bree was held."

Jamie shook her head. "They burned the place to the ground. Kirk told me that when he called to threaten me to stay silent."

Hell. But still a burned-out house was better than nothing. "I want the address, anyway," Kade insisted. He'd get a CSI team out there ASAP. Maybe they could find something that would give them clues about the identity of Kirk's boss.

Of course, the biggest clue might be sitting in front of them.

When Jamie finished writing the address, he took the note paper but kept staring at her. "I want those surveillance backups."

"I can't. I told you they're my insurance so that Kirk's boss won't kill me." Jamie yanked off her glasses, and he could see that her eyes were red. Maybe from crying. Kade had to consider that she was truly afraid, but he couldn't put that above Leah's and Bree's safety.

"You can give them to us." Bree also moved closer to the woman. "And you will. In exchange we'll provide you with protection."

Jamie jumped to her feet. "You can't protect me. No one can. My advice is for both of you to leave town for a while. Get lost somewhere and enjoy the time with your baby. Because as long as you continue this investigation, the danger will be there for all of us."

She turned as if to walk away, but Kade stepped in

front of her. "The backups," he reminded her. "I won't let you leave until you tell us where they are."

The threat was real and had no sooner left his mouth when he caught the movement out of the corner of his eye. Something in the trees. And it wasn't the spot where Mason had said he would be. This was farther down by the end of the pond.

Bree must have noticed it, too, because her head turned in that direction. "Get down!" she yelled.

But Kade was already moving. He latched onto Bree and Jamie and dragged them down with him. It wasn't a second too soon.

A bullet sliced across the top of the wooden table above them.

Chapter Twelve

Bree didn't take the time to berate herself for coming to this meeting in such an open place, but she might do that later. However, the bullet meant Kade and she were in a fight for their lives.

Again.

Since Kade was already holding Jamie and her, Bree drew her weapon and scrambled forward, using the table for cover. It wasn't much, but it was the nearest thing. The trees and their vehicles were yards away.

Mason, too.

Though maybe Mason was already trying to figure out how to stop what was happening.

Another bullet bashed into the table. Then another, until they were coming nonstop. Jamie screamed with each one and covered her head with her hands.

Kade turned, took aim in the direction of the shooter and fired.

Bree was ready to do the same, but Jamie's screams got louder, and the woman tried to bolt from the table. She probably thought she could make it to her car that was parked nearby. But Bree knew that once Jamie was out in the open, she'd become an easy target.

"The shots are going over us," Kade mumbled.

Somehow, Bree managed to hear him over the noise

of the shots, Jamie's screams and the sound of her own heartbeat pounding in her ears. She listened and watched.

Kade was right.

The first two shots had gone into the table, but these were much higher.

Bree kept a grip on Jamie's arm, and she looked where the bullets were landing. In the trees near Kade's truck and Jamie's car.

"He's not shooting at us," Bree said. If Jamie heard her, it didn't stop the woman from struggling.

There was another shot. Different from the others. From the sound of it, it had come from a rifle.

Mason.

Thank heaven. Because the shooter stopped firing.

Bree shifted so she could try to see what was going on, but in the shift, Jamie threw off Bree's grip. She reached for the woman again, but Jamie bolted out from beneath the table.

"Get down!" Bree yelled to her.

Jamie didn't listen to that, either. She got to her feet and started running to her car.

She didn't make it far.

Another shot tore through the air, and Bree watched in horror as it smacked into Jamie. The woman screamed and fell to the ground.

Bree didn't think. She started toward Jamie, but she felt Kade put a hard grip on her shoulder.

"No. You can't," he insisted.

And Bree knew he was right. If she went out there, she'd be shot, too. In fact, that was probably what the shooter wanted her to do.

Bree waited and watched while Jamie squirmed on the ground and clutched her left arm. There was blood, but thankfully it didn't appear to be too much. And the wound seemed to be limited to her arm. Still, she needed medical attention.

"I need your phone," Bree told Kade.

With his attention fastened on the area around the shooter, he retrieved it from his pocket and handed it to her. She called the emergency dispatcher to request backup and an ambulance.

"Stay down," Bree called out to Jamie the second she finished the call. Maybe, just maybe, Jamie would listen this time.

"No more shots," Bree heard Kade say.

He was right. There hadn't been another shot since the one that injured Jamie. And that meant either Mason had managed to neutralize the shooter or...

The thought had no sooner crossed her mind when Kade's phone buzzed. "It's Mason," Bree said.

"Answer it," Kade instructed since he was still keeping watch.

Bree pressed the answer button.

"He's getting away," Mason said. "I'm in pursuit through the east side of the park."

Oh, God.

This wasn't over.

"I heard," Kade let her know, and he moved out from beneath the table. "Stay with Jamie. I'm going after this SOB."

Kade kept low, starting away from Bree and Jamie, and he headed for the area around the pond where Mason had said he was in pursuit.

It was a risk.

And he had to do this in such a way that he could

still keep watch to make sure the shooter didn't double back and come after them again.

Specifically Jamie, since she seemed to be the target this time around.

He hoped her injuries weren't life-threatening, and while he was hoping, he added that the ambulance would be there soon. Backup, too.

Kade didn't want to leave Bree and her without as much protection as possible, but if Mason and he could catch this gunman then that could put them one step closer to making an arrest.

Behind him, Jamie was still yelling, and he could also hear sirens in the distance. Thank God. Kade threw a quick glance over his shoulder. Bree had stayed put under cover of the table, and she had her gun aimed and ready.

Good.

Kade followed along the edge of the pond. It wouldn't save him, but if the gunman started firing again, at least he could dive into the water. He hoped it wouldn't come down to that. Bree had already had enough shots fired near her today. Jamie, too.

He saw movement in the trees but didn't fire. Good thing, because it was Mason. His brother motioned to his right and then disappeared into the trees.

Kade hurried.

Mason was a good cop, but he didn't want him facing down a professional hit man on his own.

If that's what the shooter was.

Something wasn't right about all of this, but Kade couldn't put his finger on exactly what was wrong.

Kade heard the ambulance come to a stop behind him so that meant Jamie would soon have the medical care she needed. Added to that, the gunman hadn't fired in minutes so he was probably trying to get out of the area. Not stopping to take aim.

Neither did Kade.

He broke into a full run to the spot where he'd seen Mason. No sign of him yet, but he zigzagged his way through the trees and underbrush. Kade knew what was on the other side of the trees.

The back parking lot.

He listened for the sound of a car engine, but Kade couldn't hear anything over his own heavy breath and the sirens from both the ambulance and a deputy's car. Kade shoved aside some low hanging branches and ran out into a clearing that led to a hill.

Mason was there.

He had his left hand bracing his right wrist, and his gun was aimed at the parking lot.

His brother fired.

That made Kade run even faster. He barreled up the hill and caught just a glimpse of the black car before it disappeared around a bend in the road.

Mason cursed.

Kade did the same.

"Did you get a look at him?" Kade asked.

Mason cursed again and shook his head. "He was wearing a ski mask." He pulled out his phone and hit a button. A moment later, Kade heard the emergency dispatcher answer. "The assailant is driving a late model black Chevy on Elmore Road. He's armed and dangerous."

Kade knew the dispatcher would send out all available deputies to track down this guy, but he also knew it would only be a matter of minutes before the shooter reached the interstate. Once there, he'd be much harder to find.

"I'll do everything I can to catch up with him," Mason promised, and he started running toward the road where he'd no doubt left his truck.

Kade would have liked to go in pursuit, as well, but with the shooter already out of sight, he had to check on Bree and Jamie. He could still see through the trees, but he wouldn't breathe easier until he'd talked to Bree.

He made his way back through the wooded area and came out at the pond. There was a lot of activity already going on. An ambulance and two cruisers, one of which was speeding away—hopefully out to search for the shooter.

But Kade picked through all the chaos to find Bree.

She was there, next to the medics who were lifting Jamie onto a stretcher. Bree spotted him, and she hurried toward Kade, meeting him halfway. She went straight into his arms.

Right where Kade needed her to be.

"Are you okay?" she asked in a whisper.

He nodded. "You?"

"Okay."

But he checked her just in case. No signs of injury, thank goodness.

Kade automatically brushed a kiss on her forehead, looped his arm around her and went to the medic, Tommy Watters, who was strapping Jamie onto the stretcher.

Jamie's face was paper-white, and she was shaking from head to toe. "Did you catch him?" she asked Kade.

"No. But Mason is after him. We might get lucky."

Jamie groaned, and tears spilled down her cheeks. "You can't rely on luck. You have to catch him because he nearly killed me."

Kade assured her they would do everything to find

the shooter, and he turned to Tommy. "How is she?" Kade asked.

"Not bad. Looks like a flesh wound to me." The young medic followed Kade's gaze to those straps that Tommy was adjusting. "All this is just safety procedures. I'll take her straight to the hospital and have the E.R. doc check her."

"We need to be there in case the doctor releases her," Kade whispered to Bree.

She nodded, and they hurried to his truck. Later, there'd be a ton of paperwork to do—there always was when it came to a shooting—but it could wait. Jamie had said a lot of things, made a lot of accusations, and Kade didn't want her slipping away before she told them the whereabouts of those missing surveillance backups.

They got into his truck and followed right behind the ambulance as the siren wailed.

"You're sure you're okay?" Kade asked when Bree didn't say anything. She kept checking the area all around them. "Because I think that gunman is long gone."

"I agree." She squeezed her eyes shut a moment. "But I also think something about this wasn't right. The gunman wasn't really shooting at us. He kept the shots high despite the fact Jamie was under that table with us."

Yeah. Kade's thoughts were going in the same direction. "What are you thinking?"

"I hope I'm wrong, but maybe Jamie set all of this up to make herself look innocent."

Again, his thoughts were right there with Bree. "If so, it was working. Still is. After all, she got shot. That's a way to take blame off yourself."

Bree nodded. "But I watched her when you were running after the shooter, and she was stunned. And angry. I know people have a lot of reactions to being wounded, but something about this felt like a setup."

Kade made a sound of agreement. "Maybe we can press her for more info while she's at the hospital."

If her injuries were as minor as the medic seemed to think. If they weren't, then Bree and he would have to rethink their theory about this being a setup.

Kade stopped his truck in the hospital parking lot and got out, but he'd hardly made it a step when he saw the man walking toward them.

Anthony.

Kade stepped in front of Bree and slapped his hand on his gun.

Anthony held up his hands in mock surrender, but didn't stop until he was only a few feet away. He hitched his thumb to the ambulance that had stopped directly in front of the E.R. doors.

"I was at the sheriff's office when the call came in about the shooting," Anthony said. "Who's hurt?"

Kade considered being petty and not answering, but Anthony would learn it sooner or later. "It's Jamie. She was shot."

Anthony made a sound of stark surprise and dropped back a step. He looked at the medics as they lifted Jamie out of the ambulance and whisked her into E.R.

"Is she alive?" Anthony asked.

"Yes," Kade and Bree answered in unison.

It was Bree who continued. "In fact, according to the medic she'll pull through just fine." She stared at Anthony. "Bet you're all torn up about that."

His stark surprise turned to narrowed eyes. "I don't wish Jamie any harm, but she was a fool to think she could trust my father. Or Agent Cooper."

Bree huffed and folded her arms over her chest. "And you think one of them is responsible for this?"

"Who else?"

"You," Kade quickly provided. And he silently added Jamie's name to that list of possibilities.

"You're wasting your time trying to pin any of this on me." Anthony tapped his chest. "I've told you who's behind all of this, and yet both are still out on the streets. How many more shootings will it take for you to haul my father and his lackey FBI friend in for questioning?"

Right now, speaking to Jamie was his priority.

"Come on." Kade slipped his arm around Bree and started for the E.R. entrance.

"Jamie accused me of all of this, didn't she?" Anthony called out. "I'll bet she said she had some kind of proof of my wrongdoing. But let me guess, she didn't have that proof with her."

Kade and Bree stopped, and Kade eased back around to face him. Not because he wanted to see Anthony, but he wanted to make sure the man wasn't about to pull a gun on them.

"She doesn't have proof of anything," Anthony went on, "unless it's crimes she committed."

"I thought Jamie and you were friends of sorts," Kade reminded him.

"No. She's a viper. My advice? Watch your back around her, and don't believe a word she says."

Kade didn't intend to believe any of them, and this conversation was over. Even though Anthony continued to bark out warnings, Kade and Bree went to the E.R. and entered through the automatic doors.

The first person Kade saw was Tommy Watters, and he made a beeline toward them. "The shooting victim is in the examining room."

Good. Maybe it wouldn't take long, and then Kade could get Bree out of there. Even though she'd been stellar under fire, the spent adrenaline was obviously getting to her. It was getting to him, too. Besides, he needed to call Grayson and check on Leah.

Kade didn't stay in the waiting area since he wanted to keep an eye on Jamie and talk to the doctor about her injury. He led Bree past the reception desk and into the hall where there were examining rooms on each side. The first was empty. The second had a sick-looking kid with some very worried parents by his bedside.

Bree walked ahead of him, checking the rooms on the other side of the hall. She made it to the last one and whirled around.

"Where's Jamie?" she asked.

That was not a question Kade wanted to hear, and he started his own frantic search of the room. He cursed.

Because Jamie was nowhere in sight.

Chapter Thirteen

Bree had no idea what to think about this latest mess. Had Jamie left on her own, or had she been coerced into leaving the hospital?

Unfortunately, Kade and she didn't know the answer.

But after a thorough search of the area and the entire hospital, they hadn't been able to find the woman. Heck, they hadn't even been able to find anyone who'd even seen her. Jamie had simply vanished.

And without her, they couldn't get those backups.

Bree had pinned her hopes on the backups. Kade's latest phone call was to his brother Mason, who still was at the hospital reviewing the surveillance feed of the two newly installed cameras. One in the hospital parking lot. The other, fixed at the E.R. entrance where just weeks earlier someone had left Leah. It was because of Leah's abandonment that the city had put the cameras in place.

Kade was seated at Mason's desk at the sheriff's office, the phone sandwiched between his ear and shoulder, while he fired off messages to the rangers that he'd asked to assist in the search for Jamie. That's because all the deputies were tied up either providing protection for Leah and the others or investigating the shooting.

Bree had personally verified the protecting Leah part

because, despite the need to find Jamie, she had an even greater need to make sure her baby was okay. Grayson, his wife and both sisters-in-law had assured Bree that all was well, but she wouldn't be convinced of that until she held Leah in her own arms.

Kade hung up the phone and shook his head.

Bree's hopes went south for a quick end to this.

"Nothing," Kade verified. "The camera angles are wrong to film someone leaving out the side exits."

Which Jamie had no doubt done since one of those side exits was very close to the examining room where the EMT had left her to wait for the doctor.

"What about the backups?" Bree asked. "Has SAPD had time to search her house for them?"

"They're there now, but they haven't found anything so far."

She groaned even though the search had been a long shot. Her house was probably the last place Jamie would have left them. But where could they be?

"The rangers and deputies will keep looking for Jamie and the shooter," Kade continued. "And we'll look for a money trail. If she's going into hiding, she'll need cash."

Bree rubbed the back of her neck and the pain that was starting to make its way to her head. "She'll need money if she left voluntarily."

Kade nodded, stood and went to her. He took over the neck massage. At first, it felt too intimate for his brother's office—for any place—but after a few strokes of those clever fingers, Bree heard herself sigh.

"Thanks," she mumbled.

"Why don't we get out of here so you can get some rest? Maybe we can do another video call to Grayson and check on Leah."

Until he added that last part, Bree had been about to say no, that they needed to stay and assist with the search and investigation. But she was tired, and more than that, she wanted to see her daughter's face.

Bree walked into the hall, but the sound of footsteps had her turning in the direction of the dispatcher's desk.

Coop was there.

And judging from his expression, he was not a happy man.

Great. Something else to add to her already nightmare of a day.

"The dispatcher's trying to stop me from seeing you," Coop called out. He nudged the woman aside, flashing his badge, and he headed right for Bree.

"I heard about the shooting," Coop said. "Are you both all right?"

"Fine," Kade said and stayed right by her side. "The deputies have things under control so Bree and I were about to leave."

"I have to talk to Bree first." Coop's tone was definitely all FBI. Oh, yes. This would not be fun.

"About what?" she asked. Bree didn't even try to take the impatience out of her tone. She really wanted out of there now and didn't want to go another round of pressure from Coop.

Coop, however, didn't budge. "You haven't called, and I thought I made it clear that you had a decision to make."

Oh, that.

Bree hadn't forgotten that Coop had ordered her into work, but there hadn't been time. "Put me on unpaid leave," she suggested.

But Coop only shook his head. "I've been keeping the powers that be off your back, but I can't do it any longer, Bree. They want you in for some evaluations—both physical and mental. You have to come with me *now*."

"Now?" Kade and she asked in unison.

Coop lifted his shoulder. "I warned you this could happen."

"Did you tell those powers that be that Bree is assisting with an investigation?" Kade fired back. "And that she's in danger?"

"Part of the reason she's in danger is because she's here with you." Coop's mouth tightened. "If she'd come into headquarters when I asked, she wouldn't have had shots fired at her."

When Kade tried to maneuver himself in front of her, maybe to take a verbal swing at Coop, Bree positioned herself so that she was face-to-face with Coop. There was no need for Kade's career to suffer from this.

"My daughter is in danger," Bree stated as clearly as she could to Coop. "I don't have time to go to headquarters for evals."

"Then you leave me no choice." Coop held out his hand. "Surrender your badge. Because if you don't come with me, you're no longer an FBI agent."

Bree's breath stalled in her lungs. Those were words she'd certainly never expected to hear. Not from Coop, not from anyone. The badge and her job had been her life for so long now that they were *her*.

"You can't do this to her," Kade insisted.

Coop shook his head. "She's given me no choice. But Bree can fix it all just by coming with me now."

If she went to headquarters, she'd get caught in the whirlwind of paperwork and evals. There wouldn't be time to search for Jamie or those backups. There wouldn't be time for a video call to see Leah.

Bree suddenly felt drained and overwhelmed, but she knew exactly what she had to do. She took her badge from her pocket.

And handed it to Coop.

Coop's tight jaw went slack, and he just stared at her. Kade didn't say anything, either, but he gave her a questioning look.

"I'm sure," she said to Kade. "Let's go."

"You can't just go!" Coop practically shouted. He latched onto her arm, his grip hard and punishing. "You can't throw your life away like this."

Kade moved to do something about that grip, but Bree didn't want a fight to start, so she glared first at the grip and then at Coop.

"You asked for my badge and you got it. You're no longer my boss, and you'd better get your hand off me."

Coop let go of her, shook his head and stepped back. He added some raw profanity, too, and turned that profanity on Kade. "You've brainwashed her. Or else she's still too high on drugs to know what she's saying."

Bree had to fight not to slap him. "I'm not high. I'm tired—of you and this conversation." She headed for the back door and hoped Kade would follow rather than slug Coop.

With his voice low and dangerous, Kade said something to Coop, and she finally heard Kade's footsteps behind her. Thank goodness. She'd had enough violence for today. For the rest of her life.

"I'm sorry," Kade said, catching up with her. He hooked his arm around her waist. "I'll call my boss at headquarters and have him intervene. You'll get your badge back."

"Thanks, but I'm not sure I want it back." And Bree was surprised to realize that was true.

"You're a good agent," Kade pointed out.

"I *was*." She didn't say more until they had gone outside and were in Kade's truck. "But I can't go back to being a Jane. You said it yourself—motherhood and being a deep-cover operative aren't compatible."

"I said that because I didn't want to lose custody of Leah." He groaned, started his truck and headed toward the ranch.

"It's true," Bree insisted. "Besides, I'd like to take some time off and work out things in my head. And with you."

His eyebrow slid up.

"Not that way," she answered. But then she shrugged. Yes, maybe that way. "I have some savings," Bree went on. "I'm thinking about finding an apartment or a small house to rent in Silver Creek. That way I can be close to Leah." And Kade. But she kept that last part to herself.

Kade stayed quiet several moments. "You could stay at the ranch."

It was a generous offer but one she couldn't take. "Probably not a good idea while we're trying to work things out."

Several more quiet moments. "You could marry me."

Bree turned her head toward him so quickly that her neck popped. "What?"

"It makes sense. You could live at the ranch, and you wouldn't have to work. We could raise Leah together."

Bree just stared at him. "A marriage of convenience?" She shook her head. "Or more like a kept woman." Because in all of that, Kade darn sure hadn't mentioned anything about a real marriage.

"Just think about it," he snarled.

She didn't have to think about it. There was only one reason she would ever marry, and it was for love.

Period. And Kade obviously didn't love her because there'd been no mention of it.

Bree didn't love him, either.

But she was falling hard for him in spite of his making stupid, generous offers like the one he'd just made.

She mentally cursed herself. Falling for Kade would only make this more complicated. She didn't need a broken heart on top of everything else.

With the snarl still tightening his mouth, Kade took the turn toward the ranch. Where they'd likely be *alone* inside the house. Bree hadn't given that much thought, but she thought about it now—after his offer. She didn't want a fake marriage from Kade, but she did want *him*. And that meant being alone under the same roof with him wouldn't be easy.

His phone buzzed, and he put the call on speaker as he pulled to a stop in front of the house.

"This is Sgt. Garrett O'Malley at SAPD. Your brother asked me to call you."

"You found Jamie Greer?" Kade immediately asked.

"No. But we searched a storage facility that Ms. Greer had rented, and we got lucky. We found the surveillance backups that were missing from the Fulbright Clinic investigation."

Chapter Fourteen

Kade sat on the foot of his bed and waited for Bree to finish her shower. She'd been in there awhile, and he figured she wouldn't end it anytime soon.

Probably because she was trying to work out what had happened.

Kade could still see the look on Bree's face when Coop had demanded her badge and when she'd handed it to him. Coop had given her no choice, but that didn't mean Bree wasn't hurting. And Kade was hurting for her. The badge was a big part of who they were, and it had no doubt cost her big-time to surrender it.

Kade could also still see Bree's face when he'd suggested they get married. The timing had sucked, of course. And he hadn't meant to blurt it out like that. But it was something that had been on his mind since she'd first arrived at the ranch. While a marriage of convenience didn't sound ideal, it was a way for both of them to raise Leah and not have to deal with split custody.

Still, he'd made it seem more like a business merger rather than a proposal.

The question was—would Bree take him up on it?

He groaned, moved his laptop to the nightstand and dropped back on the bed. Kade was too afraid to close his eyes even for a minute because as tired as he was, he might fall asleep. To say the day had been long was a massive understatement.

It wasn't just the proposal. There'd been the meeting with Jamie. The shooting and her disappearance from the hospital. The confrontations with both Anthony and Coop. Followed by SAPD recovering those backups. They were in the process of reviewing them, and the sergeant had told Kade that once they finished the initial review, the backups would be delivered to the ranch by courier in a couple of hours.

It would take more than a couple of hours to go through them.

Maybe all night.

That's why Bree and he had gone ahead with the video call to Grayson and Leah before her shower. Their daughter had slept through the entire call, but it'd been good to see her precious little face.

When the bathroom door opened, Kade snapped back up and tried to look alert. Suddenly, it wasn't that hard to do when he caught sight of Bree. Fresh from her shower, her hair was damp. Her face, too. And the heat and steam had put color back in her cheeks.

No pink pjs but she was wearing a pink bathrobe that hit well above her knees.

"Darcy must have a thing for pink clothes," Bree said apologetically.

Obviously. And even though it wasn't Bree's usual color, it looked good on her. Too good. Especially the parts of her that the robe didn't cover. Those parts were the ones that latched onto his attention.

"Darcy said it was okay to check her closet." Bree fluttered her hand toward the doorway. "So, I thought I'd look for a pair of jeans."

She took a step but then stopped. Stared at him. "Is

something wrong? Is there a problem with the back-ups?"

"No problem." He stood, and to give his hands something to do, he crammed them into his jeans pockets. "They should be here in a couple of hours."

Hours, as in plenty of time to do something about whatever it was that was happening between them.

Bree nodded.

Kade figured the best thing to do would be to keep his distance from Bree. The air between them was changing. Heating up from warm to hot. He blamed it in part on the clingy bathrobe, but the truth was, Bree could be wearing anything and he would have had the same reaction.

Heck, he'd reacted to her while they were under-cover.

She stood there, staring at him. Waiting, maybe. Kade didn't make her wait long. He started toward her just as Bree started toward him.

He pulled her into his arms.

The kiss was instant, hungry, as if they were starved for each other. That wasn't too far from the truth. Kade had wanted her for a long time now.

He eased back just a fraction to make sure she wasn't planning to stop this. She wasn't. Bree hooked her arms around him and pulled Kade right back to her.

The fire slammed through him. The need, too. And he knew he had lost any chance of looking at this with reason and consequences. Sex wasn't about reason. It was about the burning need to take this woman that had turned him inside out.

"Kade," she whispered with her mouth against his. It wasn't a soft romantic purr, either. There was an urgency to it.

Something Kade understood because he felt the same urgency.

They fell backward onto the bed, and the kiss continued. So did the fight to get closer. Body to body.

Kade took those kisses to her neck. And lower. He snapped open the robe and kissed her breasts. Bree arched her back, moving closer, and she made a sound of pure feminine pleasure.

A sound that kicked up the urgency a notch.

"Now," Bree insisted.

She meant it, too. She went after his shirt, pulling the buttons from their holes and shoving it off his shoulders. It was easier for Kade. All he had to do was pull off that robe, and underneath was a naked woman.

Well, almost.

Bree wore just a pair of white panties, and Kade would have quickly rid her of those if she hadn't played dirty. She ran her hand down his bare chest. To his stomach.

And below.

That crazy frantic touch let him know exactly what she wanted.

Kade turned her, rolling on top of her so he could work his way out of his jeans. Bree didn't help with that, either. She kept kissing him. Kept touching. Until he was certain he'd go crazy. But somehow, he managed to get off his boots and Wrangler jeans.

"Hold that thought," he mumbled when she dropped some kisses on his chest.

He leaned across to the nightstand and took out a condom. Good thing he remembered. With the fire burning his mind and body, and with Bree pulling him closer and closer, he was surprised he could remember anything, including his name.

Bree pulled him back to her the moment he had the condom on, and Kade landed with his body on hers. Perfect. Or not. Bree maneuvered herself on top, and in the same motion she took him inside her.

No more frantic touches or kisses.

Both stilled a moment, and their gazes met.

Kade saw the surprise in her eyes and figured she saw it in his. He'd expected this to be good. But not this good. This felt like a lot more than sex.

She started to move, rocking against him and creating the contact they needed to make that fire inside him flame high. The need built. Little by little. With each of the strokes inside her. However, even through his sex-hazed mind, Kade took a moment to savor the view.

Oh, man.

Bree was beautiful.

He'd known that, of course, but this was like a fantasy come true.

She pushed herself against him. Harder and faster. Until Kade felt her shatter. His own body was on the edge, begging for release, but still he watched her. He watched as Bree went right over the edge.

"Kade," she said. This time, it was a purr.

And he gathered her in his arms, pushed into her one last time and let himself go.

BREE COULDN'T CATCH HER breath, and she wasn't sure she cared about such things as breathing.

Every part of her was on fire but yet slack and sated.

At peace.

Strange. She'd thought that sex with Kade would cause immense pleasure followed by the feeling that they'd just screwed things up worse than they already were.

Well, the pleasure had been immense all right.

Maybe it would take a while for the screwed-up feeling to set in.

But for now, she would just pretend that all was right with the world while they lay there naked and in each other's arms.

Kade made a lazy, satisfied sound. A rumble deep within his throat, and as if it were something they did all the time, he pulled her against him and kissed her. The moment was magic. Perfect. And even though Bree tried to keep the doubts and demons at bay, she couldn't stop the thoughts from coming. Well, one thought, anyway.

What now?

She couldn't accept his marriage proposal. Yes, she cared for Kade. Was hotly attracted to him and vice versa. But that wasn't the basis for a real marriage. For that matter, neither was the fact that they had a child together.

Kade made another of those sounds, gave her another kiss. "I'll be right back." And he headed into the bathroom.

The walk there was interesting, and she got a good look at his backside. Oh, yeah. The man was hot, and that body appealed to her in a down-and-dirty kind of way. Too bad the rest of him appealed to her, as well.

Because this could lead to a crushed heart for her.

With that miserable idea now in her head, Bree got up, located her bathrobe and slipped it on. She was trying to locate her panties when the bathroom door opened, and Kade came back in the room.

Naked.

She got a good frontal view this time and went all

hot again. Mercy. She'd just had him. How could she want him this much again so soon?

His eyebrow lifted in not an approving way at the bathrobe.

"The backups will arrive soon," she reminded him. It was the truth, but it was that fear of a crushed heart that had her putting on the terry cloth armor.

He frowned, walked to her and pulled her back onto the bed. Kade also slipped his hand into the robe and cupped her breast. "We have at least another hour," he drawled. "My suggestion? We stay naked."

Bree laughed before she could stop herself.

And just like that, the moment was perfect again. No doubts. No worries of hearts. Kade sealed the moment with another of those searing, mind-draining kisses that reminded her that yes, they were indeed naked. Or almost. He shoved open the robe and kissed his way down from her mouth to her stomach.

At first Bree thought the sound was the buzzing in her head, but when Kade cursed, she realized it was his phone.

He rolled off the bed, grabbed his jeans from the floor and jerked out his phone. He glanced at the screen and shook his head.

"The caller blocked the number," Kade mumbled, and he put the call on speaker. "Special Agent Ryland."

"Agent Ryland," the person answered.

And with just those two words, Bree's blood turned to ice. Because it wasn't a normal voice. The caller was speaking through a voice scrambler.

"Who is this?" Kade demanded.

"Someone you're going to meet in an hour at the Fulbright Clinic in San Antonio."

The voice sounded like a cartoon character, making

it impossible to recognize the speaker. But that didn't mean she couldn't figure out who it was. After all, there weren't many people who would make a demand like that.

"The Fulbright is closed," Kade reminded the caller. "It's an abandoned building now."

"Yes." The caller paused. "And that's exactly why it's a good place for us to meet. Show up in one hour alone. Just you and Bree. And when you come, bring those missing surveillance backups with you."

Kade glanced back at her and groaned softly. This was no doubt one of their suspects. But which one? McClendon, Anthony, Jamie?

Or heaven forbid, Coop?

"We don't have the backups," Kade said.

"Yes, but you can get them from SAPD. And trust me, it'll be in your best interest to get them and bring them to me at the clinic."

The caller didn't raise his voice, didn't change his inflection, but the threat slammed through her.

"Leah," she mouthed.

Kade shook his head, pulled her down to him and whispered in her ear, "Grayson would have called if something had gone wrong with Leah."

True. If something hadn't gone wrong with Grayson, too. Maybe the missing shooter or one of the suspects had gotten into the estate and was holding them all captive.

"Call him," Kade whispered, and he pointed to the house phone on the nightstand next to Kade's laptop. And he mouthed the number.

"It won't do any good to try to trace this call," the voice on the phone said. "Prepaid cell. And I'll toss it once we're done here."

Bree kept one ear tuned to what was being said, but she grabbed the house phone and went to the other side of the room. Grayson answered on the first ring.

"Is Leah okay?" she whispered.

"Of course. Why? What's wrong?"

The breath swooshed out of Bree, and the relief nearly brought her to her knees. "Are you all okay? Is anyone there threatening you?"

"Not a chance. I have this place locked up tight with Nate and Dade standing guard. Why?"

Bree couldn't get into details, mainly because she had to figure out what exactly the details were. "We might have a problem. Kade will call you when he can." And she hung up so they could finish this puzzling call.

"Leah's okay," she relayed in a whisper to Kade.

The relief was quick and obvious.

"Give me one reason," he said to the caller, "why Bree and I would meet you and give you evidence?"

"One reason?" the person repeated. "Oh, I have a big one reason. Well, actually a small one, but I think it'll be a very big reason to Bree and you. Check your email."

Bree's heart was still pounding like crazy, and she wanted to dismiss all of this as some kind of ploy, but that didn't stop Kade and her from moving toward his laptop. It was already on so he clicked into his email and found a new one with an attachment.

"Click onto the link in the attachment," the caller ordered.

Kade did, and the link took them to an online video. One with very poor quality. It appeared to be a dark room, so dark that Bree couldn't make out anything in it.

"Let me move closer to the camera," the caller said.

There was the sound of footsteps. Still no light. But

as the footsteps got louder, she could just make out the image of someone. An adult. The person was cloaked in black. Maybe a cape with a hood. And the person was seated in a chair.

He or she was holding something.

Bree drew in her breath. Waited. And zoomed in on whatever was in the person's arms.

Oh, God.

It was a baby.

"Leah!" she practically screamed when she saw the baby's face.

"It's not her," Kade said, but he didn't sound convinced. "It's some kind of trick."

Yes. Bree forced herself to remember that Grayson had just told her that Leah was all right. Kade's brother wouldn't have lied, and he hadn't sounded under duress when he'd answered her.

"No trick," the caller assured them, the cartoon voice sounding smug. "But the baby isn't Leah."

Bree shook her head. It was a real baby all right. Dressed in a pink dress and wrapped in a pink blanket, she was asleep, but Bree could see the face.

A face identical to Leah's.

"Confused?" the caller mocked. "Well, I've been keeping a little secret. And the secret is the reason you'll both come alone to the clinic and bring me those tapes."

"Who's baby is that?" Kade demanded.

The caller laughed. "Yours. Yours and Bree's," he corrected.

"What?" Bree managed to say. She had no choice but to drop down onto the bed.

Kade didn't look too steady, either. "What do you mean?"

"I mean seven weeks ago, Bree gave birth to identical twin girls."

"Oh, God," Bree mumbled, and because she didn't know what else to do, she kept repeating it.

She stared at the face, at the shadows, and could only shake her head. What was going on?

"Here's the bottom line," the caller continued, the horrible voice pouring through the room. "If you don't want your second daughter to be sold on the black market, then you'll be here alone at the clinic in one hour. I'll trade the baby for the backups."

Chapter Fifteen

"Wait!" Kade shouted into the phone.

But it was too late. The caller had already hung up. And his computer screen went blank. Someone had pulled the plug on the video feed.

Behind him, Bree was gasping and shaking her head.

"It is possible?" Kade asked. "Could you really have had twins?"

She looked at him, her eyes filled to the brim with tears. "I suppose so. They sedated me for the C-section."

Kade cursed. Yes, it was possible this could be some kind of elaborate hoax, but it was too big of a risk to take to ignore it.

He wiped away her tears. "Get dressed. We're going after the baby."

Bree nodded, and even though she was shaky, she hurried to the bathroom where she'd left her clothes. Kade dressed, too, and he called his brother Grayson.

"We have a problem," Kade said when Grayson answered. "I don't have time to sugarcoat this or explain it other than to say I need those surveillance backups from SAPD. Someone called and wants the backups in exchange for a baby. A twin girl that Bree might have delivered when she had Leah."

"What?" Grayson snapped.

Kade ignored his brother's shock and the questions Grayson likely wanted answered now. "Just have an SAPD officer, one you can trust, meet us at the intersection of Dalton and Reyes in San Antonio."

"The Fulbright Clinic is near there. Kade, you're not thinking—"

"Bree and I have to go in alone. That's the condition."

Grayson cursed. "But it could be dangerous. It could be a trap."

Both of those were true. "What would you do if it were your child?" Kade fired back.

Grayson cursed again. "At least let me arrange to have some backup in the area."

"Only if they stay far away and out of sight. I'm figuring this guy has already set up some kind of perimeter surveillance. They'll know if we have someone with us."

"Who did this?" Grayson pressed.

"When I know, I'll you let know. For now, just get me those backups."

Kade ended the call, knowing his brother would make it happen. After all, his other brother Nate, was an SAPD lieutenant, and he could do whatever it took to have those backups ready and waiting for them.

He hurried, dressing as fast as he could, and by the time he'd finished, Bree ran out of the bathroom. Dressed and looking ready to panic.

"We can do this," he promised her and hoped it wasn't a lie.

Kade put on his shoulder holster and ankle strap, filled both with guns and extra ammunition, and he took his backup weapon from the nightstand and handed it to Bree. She also grabbed some extra magazines of bullets and stuffed them into her pockets. They couldn't go in there with guns blazing, not with a baby's safety at stake, but Kade had no plans to go in unarmed, either.

They both ran down the stairs, but Kade used the security monitor by the door to make sure no one had sneaked onto the ranch. When he was sure it was safe, they hurried outside to his truck, and he drove away fast.

"What about the backups?" she asked.

"Grayson will get them."

She nodded and made what sounded to be a breath of relief. But Kade knew neither of them would be in the relief mode until they figured out what the heck was going on.

"Think back," he told her. He flew down the ranch road and onto the route that would take them to the interstate. "When you were pregnant, did you have any indications there was more than one baby?"

"Maybe." Her forehead bunched up. "There was a lot of movement from the baby, a lot of kicking and moving around and I felt huge. But I figured plenty of pregnant women felt that way."

"They do." He'd gone through his sister-in-law's pregnancy and now Grayson's wife, and both had complained about their size. "What about an ultrasound?"

"They did one, but they didn't let me see the monitor."

Hell, probably because they hadn't wanted her to know that it was twins.

But why keep that from her?

One baby or two, Bree wasn't going to fight them back for fear of harming the child. Her captors had her exactly where they wanted her.

"The second baby is their ace in the hole," Bree mumbled. And she groaned. "I remember Kirk using that term, but I thought he was talking about me. Or Leah. I had no idea he was talking about another baby."

Kade mentally groaned, too. "What did Kirk say exactly?"

She lifted her hand in a gesture to indicate she was thinking about it. "He said it wouldn't do any good for me to escape, that he had an ace in the hole." Her gaze rifled to him. "But why would Kirk's boss wait all these weeks to tell us about the other baby?"

Unfortunately, Kade had a theory about that. "Maybe the boss thought you were dead and if so, you couldn't testify against him. When you resurfaced, that meant you became a threat."

She turned in the seat toward him. "But Jamie's the real threat because she's the one who had those backups."

He shook his head. "She wasn't a threat as long as she kept the backups hidden. After all, those backups implicated her in a crime, too. She didn't want the cops or us to have them. She wanted to hang on to them as her own ace in the hole."

Bree pulled in her breath, nodded. "Then SAPD found the backups and now all of this has come to a showdown."

A showdown where his baby could be in danger.

"Twins," he said under his breath. He had to accept that it was possible. And that meant he had to do everything humanly possible to save his child.

"I'm sorry," Bree whispered, her voice shaking hard. "I should have put all the little things together to know there was a second baby."

"You couldn't have known. This was all part of some sick plan, and keeping you in the dark was essential." He took the ramp to the interstate. "But Jamie should have known. Even if she wasn't there for your C-section, she must have heard Kirk talking to someone about it."

"Yes," Bree agreed. "So, why didn't she say anything at the park?"

Kade could think of a reason. A bad one. Maybe Jamie was the person behind all of this. Those backups could have been her protection from Kirk's boss.

Or Jamie could be the boss.

"This might be Jamie's way of getting the backups back," Kade pointed out.

Bree stayed quiet a moment and then nodded. "That would explain why we're just now getting the news of the other baby." Another pause. "There must be something incriminating that we don't know about on those backups."

Kade agreed. And the bad flip side to that was SAPD hadn't had time to review them. Neither had Kade and Bree.

"It's too big of a risk to take in fake backups," Bree said. "And we can't give him or her just one or two. This person knows how many backups there are."

She took the words right out of his mouth. No, the person would almost certainly verify they were real before he or she handed over the baby.

And then what?

Kade didn't like the scenarios that came to mind. But there was a possible good outcome.

Well, semigood.

"The person disguised his or her voice," Kade explained, playing this through in his mind. "So, it's possible we can do a safe exchange. The backups for the baby."

"And we just walk out of there," Bree added in a mumble.

Yeah. That was the best-case scenario. Kade didn't want to do any bargaining with this SOB while the baby was still in the picture. Later, once they were all out of there, he'd move Bree, the twin and Leah to another safe location.

Then, he'd go after the person who'd orchestrated this.

Of course, that was just the beginning. If the second baby was real, then he had another child. To love and raise. To protect. Another custody issue to work out with Bree.

Since all of that was only clouding his mind, he pushed it aside and focused just on now. And *now* started with getting the backups.

Kade drove into San Antonio and kept an eye on both Bree and the clock. The caller had given them only an hour to deliver the backups, and half that time was already gone. He hated to think of what would happen if they were late.

He slowed down when he reached the intersection of Dalton and Reyes, and Kade's heart nearly stopped when he didn't see anyone waiting for them. But then, his brother Nate stepped from the side of a gas station. Kade mumbled a prayer of thanks and pulled in, stopping right next to Nate.

"The backups," Nate said. He handed the evidence envelope to Kade when he lowered the window.

"Thanks." Kade dropped the envelope on the seat between Bree and him. "Did this put your badge on the line?"

Nate shrugged. Meaning, it had.

"I'm sorry," Kade told him. And he was. He knew how much the badge meant to Nate, but he also knew how much family meant to him. "Grayson told you about the baby?"

"Yeah." Nate looked over his shoulder in the direction of the Fulbright clinic only a block away. "I put some SWAT guys on the roof." He hitched his thumb to the three-story building not far from where they stood. "And I have six others waiting to respond. We haven't seen anyone outside the clinic, but we've only been here about ten minutes."

Kade mumbled another thanks, took out his phone and set it so that he could reach Nate with just the touch of one button. "What about using infrared to get a glimpse of who's inside?"

Nate shook his head. "We tried. No luck. The place used to be a radiology clinic, and infrared won't penetrate the walls."

Bree made a frustrated sound, and even though the timing sucked, Kade remembered that he hadn't introduced Bree to this particular brother. But it would have to wait.

"Be careful," Nate said, and he stepped back from the truck.

Kade nodded and drove away, making his way toward the clinic. Less than a year ago, Bree and he had to battle their way out of here and had run along this very street.

Maybe they wouldn't have to do that again.

The thought of trying to escape with a baby under those circumstances sickened him.

Bree pulled in a hard breath when Kade came to a stop in the clinic's parking lot. It was empty. Not another vehicle in sight. No lights, either. Even the ones in the parking lot were out—maybe because the caller had disabled them.

There was also a problem with the windows. Each one facing the parking lot had burglar bars. Thick metal rods jutting down the entire length of the glass. It would be impossible to use those to escape.

The moment Kade turned off the engine, his phone buzzed. The caller's info had been blocked, just like before.

"Agent Ryland," the scrambled voice greeted him when Kade answered. "So glad you made it. Do you have the backups?"

"I do," Kade hesitantly answered.

"Excellent. Both of you enter the clinic through the front door. I've already unlocked it. You're to put all your weapons and the backups on the floor—"

"I'll give you the backups when you give us the baby," Kade interrupted.

There was silence for several heart-stopping moments. "All right," the caller finally said. "Then, let's get this show on the road."

The person ended the call, and Kade looked at Bree to make sure she was up to doing this. She was. Yes, she'd cried earlier, but there weren't tears now. Just the determined face of a well-trained federal agent who would do anything to get her baby out of harm's way.

"If something goes wrong," Kade whispered, "I want you to take the baby and get out of there. I'll run interference."

She shook her head, and the agent facade waivered a bit, but she couldn't argue. The baby had to come first.

"We're all coming out of there alive," Bree whispered back. And she leaned over and kissed him.

Kade wanted to hold on to that kiss, on to her and that promise, but there wasn't time. "Stay behind me," he added, "and hide your gun in the back waist of your pants."

After she'd done that, he stepped from his truck. He waited until Bree was indeed behind him before they walked to the double front doors. He wished they were glass so he could see inside but no such luck. They were thick wood. Kade said another prayer and tested the knob.

The door opened.

Like the exterior of the building and the parking lot, the entrance was pitch-black, and he could barely make out what appeared to be a desk and some chairs. This was the reception area, and if anyone was there, he couldn't see, hear or sense them.

"Here's my gun," Kade called out, and he took his weapon and one of the extra magazines and put them on the floor.

"Now, the other weapons." The voice boomed over an intercom. The same scrambled voice as the caller.

"Weapon," Kade corrected. And he motioned for Bree to surrender her gun, as well.

Kade could feel her hesitation, but she finally did it. That only left them with the small gun in his ankle holster, and he hoped like the devil that the SOB on the intercom didn't know about it.

Behind them, there was a sharp click. Not someone cocking a gun. But maybe just as dangerous.

Someone had locked the door. That someone had no doubt used a remote control because Nate wouldn't have let anyone get close to the exterior side of the door.

"Kick the weapons down the hall," the voice ordered.

Kade did it, the sound of metal scraping across the tiled floor.

"Here," Kade whispered to Bree, and he handed her

his cell so if necessary she could make that emergency call to Nate. It would also free up his hands in case he had to go for the ankle holster.

"Where's the baby?" Kade asked, holding up the envelope with the backups.

"I'll have to verify the backups first. Walk forward, down the hall. Keep your hands in the air so I can see them at all times."

The *dark* hall. Where they could be ambushed and the backups taken from them.

"How about you meet us halfway?" Kade asked.

"How about you follow orders?" the person snapped.

"Because your orders could get us killed. Either meet us halfway, or show us the baby now."

More silence. And with each passing second, Kade's heartbeat revved up. Bree's breathing, too. Since her arm was against his back, he could feel how tense she was.

"Okay," the person finally said. "Start walking. I'll do the same."

It was a huge risk, but staying put was a risk, too.

Kade took the first step, then waited and listened. He heard some movement at the end of that dark hall, and he took another step. Then another. Bree was right behind him and hopefully would stay there.

If this goon sent in someone from behind, through those front doors, Nate's men would stop them. The same if a gunman tried to shoot through one of the windows.

So, the danger was ahead.

"There are two rooms ahead off the hall," Bree whispered. "One on the left. The other on the right."

Kade hadn't remembered that about the clinic layout, but he was thankful that Bree had. He would need to make sure no one came out of those rooms to ambush them.

Another step.

The person at the end of the hall did the same.

Now that Kade's eyes were adjusting a little to the darkness, he could see the shadowy figure better. Well, the outline of the person, anyway. He couldn't make out any feature and couldn't tell if it was a man or woman. The person seemed to be wearing some kind of dark cloak.

"When you get to the spot where the reception area meets the hall," the voice instructed, "take the backups from the envelope and hold them up so I can see them."

Kade made several more steps to get to that spot, and with his attention fastened on the figure ahead of him, he took out the backups and lifted them in the air.

Overhead on the hall ceiling, a camera whirred around, the lens angling toward Kade's hand. Either this guy had backup inside the building or else he was using a remote control device.

Kade was betting he had backup.

Behind him, he heard a buzzing sound. His phone. And Kade mentally cursed. "Answer it," he whispered to Bree, hoping that the person at the end of the hall hadn't heard.

She didn't say anything, but she pressed a button and put the phone to her ear. A moment later, she froze.

"What's wrong?" Kade asked, still trying to keep his voice low.

"You're sure?" she asked.

Kade was about to repeat his *what's wrong* question, but Bree latched onto his arm.

"It's a trap," she said. And Bree started to pull him to the floor.

But it was already too late.

The shot slammed through the air.

Chapter Sixteen

Bree pulled Kade to the right, out of the line of fire of the person in the hall.

Just as the bullet slammed into the locked door.

Kade and she slammed onto the floor. Hard. It knocked the breath right out of her, but Bree fought to regain it so she could get them out of harm's way.

If that was even possible now.

Thankfully, Kade could breathe and react because he grabbed her by the shoulder and dragged her onto the other side of the desk. He also drew the small Colt .38 from his ankle holster. It wasn't much firepower considering their situation.

And their situation was *bad*.

"Stop shooting!" Kade yelled. He shoved the backups inside his shirt. "You could hit the baby."

The person laughed, that cartoony voice echoing through the dark clinic. Bree knew the reason for the sickening laughter.

"There's no second baby?" Kade whispered to her on a rise of breath.

"Not here. That was Mason on the phone. About ten minutes ago a woman dropped off a baby at the Silver Creek hospital. A baby who looks exactly like Leah. She's all right. She hadn't been harmed."

The sound that Kade made deep in his throat was a mixture of relief and dread. Relief because their baby was all right, away from the monster who'd fired that shot at them. But the danger for Kade and she was just starting.

"Thank you for cooperating with my plan," the figure called out. "And see? I'm not such a bad person, after all. The woman I hired to take the baby to the hospital did exactly as I asked. So, all is well."

Kade cursed. "If all is truly well as you say, then you'll let us go."

"Can't do that."

Another bullet blasted into the door.

Kade's brother Nate would likely have heard the shots. He no doubt knew about the baby being dropped off at the hospital. But there was no way Nate could come in with guns blazing. Still, if Kade and she could make it to the window, they might be able to figure out a way through those burglar bars. Then Nate might be able to provide enough cover for them to get out of there.

Later, when this was over, she'd try to come to terms with the fact that the second baby was real. That she'd delivered twins. But right now, she had to focus on keeping Kade and her alive.

"You can have the backups," Bree told the shooter. She latched onto Kade and inched toward the window. "And we don't know who you are. There's no reason for you to kill us."

"Oh, there's a reason." And that's all the person said for several moments. "You both know too much. Especially you, Bree. You're too big of a risk because I have no idea what you might have overheard when Kirk was holding you. You might know who I am, and I can't risk you testifying against me."

Bree tried to figure out who was speaking. All of their suspects probably thought Kade and she knew *too much*. Especially since all their suspects were tied in some way or another to this clinic.

"I didn't overhear anything that would identify Kirk's boss," she explained, hoping the sound of her voice would cover Kade's and her movement toward the window.

"Can't take that chance," the shooter fired back.

He also fired another shot into the door.

"Oh, and if I were you, I wouldn't try to get out through the window—they're locked up tight and they have thick metal security bars. So, you might as well stop where you are. Well, unless you want his brother to die."

Oh, mercy.

Kade and she froze. The shooter must have a camera in place so that they were watching their every move.

"What the hell does my brother have to do with this?" Kade shouted.

"A lot actually. Before your cop brother arrived to put some of his men on the roof near here, I already had a gunman in place. In the catbird seat, you might say."

Kade cursed. "He could be lying," he whispered to Bree.

But it didn't sound like a lie. This person had had plenty of time to set all of this up.

"My hired gun has a rifle trained on your brother right now," the person added.

That didn't sound like a lie, either, and even if it was, it was too big a risk to take. Nate had come to help them, and she didn't want him dying.

Bree knew what she had to do. Now it was just a matter of convincing Kade to let her do it.

"I'm the threat to your identity," she shouted, levering herself up a little so that she could peer over the desk. "Not Kade. Let him go. So he can raise our daughters," Bree added so that it would remind Kade of what was at stake here.

If both of them died in this clinic, their twins would become orphans.

"You're not doing this," Kade immediately said, and he pulled her back down behind the desk.

The shooter laughed. "I'm not looking for a sacrificial lamb. I'm afraid both of you have to die."

Her stomach twisted, but Bree wasn't about to give up. There had to be some kind of argument she could use to get at least Kade out of this alive.

There was a sound. Some kind of movement at the end of the hall. And Bree tried to brace herself for the person to come closer.

Where Kade could shoot to kill.

"These are copies of the backups," she tried. "Not the originals. Those are in a safe place."

"Liar," the shooter answered.

Was it her imagination or did the person sound farther away than before?

"The backups can't be copied," the voice continued. "And I should know because it's a security check that I put in place. Didn't want anyone copying them to use them for blackmail."

"They're not coming closer," Kade whispered.

She'd been right about the moving away part. But why would the person do that?

Unless he or she was trying to escape?

But that didn't make sense, either. Kade and she had the backups.

"I'm afraid I have to say goodbye now." And footsteps followed that puzzling comment.

Was the person just leaving them there?

No, her gut told her that wouldn't happen and that something was terribly wrong.

Kade must have realized it, too, because he got to his feet and hurried to the door. He rammed his shoulder against it, but it didn't budge.

And then he cursed.

Bree stood, trying to figure out what had caused his reaction, and she spotted the tiny blinking red light on the wall. Except it wasn't just a light.

The blinks were numbers.

Ticking down.

Seven, six, five…

"It's a bomb!" Kade shouted.

He grabbed Bree and they started to run.

KADE HAD TO MAKE A split-second decision because a few seconds were all they had left.

The door behind them was locked. No way out there. It was the same with the windows. He could risk pulling Bree behind the desk, but he could see the fistful of explosives attached to the timing device. The reception area and the desk were going to take the brunt of the impact.

So, with his left hand vised around Bree's arm, he raced down that dark hall.

Yeah, it was a risk. The shooter could be waiting for them to do just that, but at the moment the bomb was a bigger risk, especially since the shooter had also made a run for it.

"Hurry!" Kade shouted to Bree, though she no doubt understood the urgency.

They raced down the hall, past the first two rooms that were nearest to the lobby, and he pulled her into the next door. He dived toward a desk, pulling her underneath it with him. Kade also put his body over hers.

The blast tore through the building.

The sound was deafening, and the blast sent debris slamming into the desk and a chunk of the wall slammed into Kade's back. He'd have a heck of a bruise, but Bree was tucked safely beneath him.

He got his gun ready, in case he had to shoot their way out of there, but the sound made him realize they had bigger things to worry about than the shooter.

The ceiling groaned, threatening to give way.

"Run!" Bree shouted.

She fought to get up, just as Kade fought to get the debris off him. They finally made it to their feet and raced out of the room. What was left of it, anyway. It was the same for the hall. Walls had collapsed, and there was junk and rubble everywhere.

Bree hurdled over some of the mess and continued down the hall. Cursing, Kade caught up with her, and shoved her behind him. Of course, that might not be any safer, what with the ceiling about to come down, but there were other rooms ahead. An exit, too. And he didn't want that shooter jumping out from the shadows.

After all, Kade still had the backups.

Maybe the guy thought the blast would destroy them, along with Bree and him. Especially Bree, since the bozo clearly thought she was the biggest threat. Still, this could be all part of some warped plan to get them out and into the open so he could gun them down.

Behind them, another chunk of the ceiling fell. It

slammed into the tile floor and sent a new spray of debris their way. They kept on running until they reached the back exit. Kade hit the handle to open it.

Hell.

It was locked.

He cursed, grabbed Bree again and ducked into the room to their left. He couldn't be sure, but he thought this would lead them to the quarters where the infertile couples stayed. As Bree and he had done. There were more exits back in that area. Maybe, just maybe, not all of them would be locked.

His phone buzzed, and since Bree was still holding it, she pressed the button to put the call on speaker.

"Are you okay?" the person asked.

Not the shooter. It was Nate.

"Barely," Kade answered. "Did you see anyone leave the building?"

"No."

Kade cursed again and kept watch around them. "Bree and I are trying to make our way to an east side exit."

"Good. My men and I are converging on the building now."

Kade wanted to ask about the baby, how she was doing after being dropped off at the hospital, but it would have to wait. Right now, he had to get Bree out of there. Bree closed the phone and they started running as fast as they could.

Her breath was gusting. His, too. They meandered their way through the maze of rooms and furniture until they came to another hall. There were more windows in this part of the building. Good thing because it allowed him to see.

There was a door ahead.

"Stay behind me," Kade reminded her once again. He lifted his gun and made a beeline to the door.

They were still a good ten feet away when the second blast ripped through the hall.

Chapter Seventeen

Bree didn't have time to get down. The blast came right at them, and she felt herself flying backward. Everything seemed in slow motion but fast, too.

Her back collided with the wall.

Kade hit the concrete block wall beside her, and despite the bone-jarring impact, he managed to hang on to his gun. He also yanked her to her feet. Kade didn't have to warn her that they had to get out of there.

She knew.

Because there had already been two explosions, and that meant there could be another.

So far Kade and she had either gotten lucky or this was all some kind of elaborate trap.

"This way," Kade said, and he led her away from the part of the hall where the door had once been. It was now just a heap of rubble—a mix of concrete, wood and metal—and it was dangerous to try to get through it.

They hurried in the other direction, back through the rooms where Kade and she had stayed nearly a year ago when they were undercover.

Each step spiked her heartbeat and tightened the knot in her stomach. Because each step could lead them straight into another explosion. For that matter, the entire place could be rigged to go up.

Kade and she made their way into another hall, one
with windows. And it was the thin white moonlight
stabbing its way through the glass that allowed Bree to
see the movement just ahead of them.

Kade pulled her into the room.

Just as a shot zinged through the air.

There was another jolt to her body when Kade
and she landed on the floor. Another shot, too. But it
slammed into the doorjamb and thankfully not them.

Despite the hard fall, Kade got her out of the doorway, and they scrambled to the far side of the room.

She glanced around. More windows, all with security bars, and there were two doors, feeding off in both
directions. The doors were closed, but that didn't mean
someone couldn't be waiting on the other side.

Since she no longer had a gun, Bree grabbed the first
thing she could reach—a metal wire wastebasket. It
wasn't much of a weapon, but if she got close enough,
she could use it to bash someone.

Another shot.

This one also took a chunk out of the doorjamb.

As unnerving at those shots were, it did give Bree
some good news. Well, temporary good news, anyway.
There likely wasn't about to be another explosion in this
area. Not with their assailant so close.

Close enough to gun them down.

"You're like cats with nine lives!" the person shouted,
still using the voice scrambler. "You should have been
dead by now."

Yes, Bree was painfully aware of that. And so was
her body. She was aching and stinging from all the cuts,
nicks and bruises. Beside her, Kade was no doubt feeling the same.

"Why don't you come in here and try to finish the job?" Kade shouted back.

Bree prayed the guy would take Kade up on the offer. Because Kade was still armed. But she didn't hear any movement in the hall or outside the building.

Were Nate and the other officers there, waiting to respond?

She hoped so because Bree didn't want this monster to escape. If that happened, the danger would start all over again. The threats to Kade and her would hang over their heads. The heads of their babies, too.

That couldn't happen.

This had to end now, tonight.

"Are you too scared to face us?" Bree yelled. Yeah, it might be a stupid move to goad their assailant, but it could work.

Maybe.

"Not scared. And I'm not stupid, either. This can only end one way—with your deaths."

"Or yours!" Bree fired back.

Kade nodded, motioned for her to keep it up, and while he kept low, he began to inch toward the hall door.

"You know, I think I do remember some things Tim Kirk said," Bree continued, keeping her voice loud to cover Kade's movement. "He wasn't very good at keeping secrets, was he?"

Silence.

Kade stopped. Waited.

"All right," their assailant finally said. "If Kirk told secrets, then who am I?" The person didn't wait for her to answer. "You don't know. You can only guess. And guessing won't help you or Agent Ryland."

Kade moved closer to the door but crouched down so that he was practically on the floor.

"What if it's not a guess?" Bree lied. "What if I've already left a sworn statement with the district attorney? Think about it—I wouldn't have risked coming here if I didn't have an ace in the hole."

She nearly choked on those words, the same ones that Kirk had used to describe her child. Maybe their attacker would recognize them and panic. Mercy, did she want panic. Maybe then the person would make a mistake, and Kade could get off that shot.

"Well?" Bree called out when she didn't get an answer. "Should I call the district attorney and tell him to release my statement?"

She waited, her heart in her throat.

Kade waited, too, his attention fastened on the hall and doorway.

Bree was so focused on what she could say to draw out this monster that she barely heard the sound. Not from the hall or the doorway.

But from behind her.

She turned and saw the shadowy figure in the now-open doorway on the right side of the room.

Oh, God.

The person lifted his arm, ready to fire. Not at her. But at Kade.

Bree didn't think. She dropped the trash can and dived at the person who was about to shoot Kade.

KADE WHIRLED AROUND just in time to see Bree launch herself at the gunman. And there was no mistaking that this was a gunman because Kade spotted the guy's weapon.

He also saw that weapon ram into Bree when she collided with their attacker. But it wasn't just the collision and the gun that latched onto his attention.

Kade's heart went to his knees when the sound of the bullet tore through the room.

"Bree!" Kade heard himself yell.

She had to be all right. If this SOB had shot her… but he couldn't go there. Couldn't bear to think of what might be. He just ran toward her.

And then he had to come to a quick stop.

Their attacker hooked an arm around Bree's throat and snapped her toward him. In the same motion, the person jammed a gun against Bree's head.

Now that Kade's eyes had adjusted to the darkness, he had no trouble seeing the stark fear on her face. Her eyes were wide, and her chest was pumping for air.

"Run!" she told Kade.

But the person ground the barrel of the gun into her temple. "If you run, she dies right now," her captor warned. "Drop your gun and give me the backups."

Kade tried to give Bree a steadying look, and then his gaze went behind her to the figure wearing the dark clothes and black ski mask. Kade also didn't miss the object in the gunman's left hand. But he or she didn't hold on to it for long.

It clattered to the floor.

The voice scrambler, Kade realized.

Their attacker had dropped it, no doubt so that both hands could be used to contain Bree. And it was working. Bree couldn't move without the risk of being either choked or shot.

"I said drop your gun and give me the backups," the man repeated.

And it was a man all right. Kade knew that now that the scrambler was no longer being used. It was a man whose voice Kade recognized.

Anthony.

So, they had the identity of the person who'd made their lives a living hell and had endangered not just them but their newborn daughters.

The anger slammed through Kade, but he tried to tamp it down because he had to figure out a way to get that gun away from Bree's head. He wasn't sure Anthony was capable of cold-blooded, close-contact murder, but considering everything else he'd likely done, it was a risk that Kade couldn't take.

"Why are you doing this, Anthony?" Bree asked, but she kept her attention fastened on Kade. Her left eyebrow was slightly cocked as if asking what she should do.

Kade didn't have an answer to that yet.

"You know why I'm doing this," Anthony assured her.

Kade heard it, but the words hardly registered. That's because he got a better look at the grip Anthony had on the gun. Oh, mercy. Anthony's hand was shaking. Not good. He was probably scared spitless despite the cocky demeanor he'd had earlier, and Kade knew from experience that scared people usually made bad decisions in situations like these.

"Put down the gun." Kade tried to keep calm. Normally, it would be a piece of cake. All those years of training and experience had taught him to disguise the fear he felt crawling through him. But this wasn't normal. Bree was on the other end of that gun.

"You don't want murder added to the list of charges," Kade pressed.

"No." And that's all Anthony said for several moments. "But I'll be charged with murder and other things if the cops see the surveillance backups."

Hell. So, that's what was on them. *Murder.* Kade figured it was bad if Anthony was willing to go through all of this to get the backups, but he'd hoped for some lesser charges. Murder meant Anthony had no way out.

This was not going to end well.

"I didn't know my father and Coop had set up the extra cameras," Anthony said, his voice shaking. "And I did some things."

Bree pulled in a hard breath, and Kade knew she'd come to the same conclusion as he had. Anthony couldn't let them out of there alive, not with those backups that could get him the death penalty.

He was a desperate man.

But Kade was even more desperate.

"I didn't know about the backups at first," Anthony went on. "I thought you and Bree were the only two people who could send me to jail."

"So you kidnapped me," Bree provided. She glanced around as if looking for a way to escape. Kade hoped she wouldn't try until he had a better shot. At the moment, he had no shot at all.

"The kidnapping worked." Anthony paused again. "Until Jamie decided to do something stupid like leaving the baby at the hospital and letting you escape." He said the woman's name like venom. "Jamie's dead now. I don't have to worry about her or her stupidity anymore."

Hell. That was not what Kade wanted to hear. Yet another confession to murder to go along with the ones on the surveillance backups.

"The cops are outside," Kade reminded him just in case Anthony had forgotten that he wasn't just going to shoot and stroll out of here.

"Yes, and so is the gunman I hired."

There was an edge in Anthony's voice. Not the edge of someone who was a hundred percent confident in this plan. So Kade decided to see if he could push a button or two.

"You mean the incompetent gunman who was supposed to kill Jamie in the park?" Kade asked.

Anthony stammered out a few syllables before he managed some full-blown profanity. Clearly the gunman was a button, and Kade had indeed managed to push it. Now he could only hope that it didn't put Bree in more danger. Kade needed Anthony distracted, not just fuming mad.

Anthony ripped off his ski mask. "Yes! That's the idiot. But he won't fail me this time. He knows it'll cost him his life if he doesn't succeed."

Kade made an *I-doubt-that* sound in his throat.

Another button push. Every muscle in Anthony's face tightened. "Give me the backups," he demanded. "And put down that gun. If I have to tell you again, you're a dead man."

Despite the *dead man* warning, Kade didn't move until he saw Antony's hand tense. He was going to pull the trigger if Kade didn't do something fast.

"Here's the gun," Kade said. He stooped down and eased it onto the floor.

Kade looked at Bree, just a split-second glance, so that she'd know he was about to try to get them out of this, and she gave a slight nod.

"Now, I want the backups," Anthony ordered.

When he was still in a crouched position, Kade reached into his shirt. But he didn't get the backups. It was now or never. He said a quick prayer and launched himself at Anthony.

Kade rammed into the man before Anthony could pull the trigger. That was the good news. But the bad news was that Bree was still in danger.

Between them.

Where Anthony could kill her.

Anthony no longer had the gun aimed at her head, but he wasn't ready to surrender. Far from it.

Kade tried to shove Bree to the side, but Anthony held on to her, choking her with the crook of his arm. She clawed at his arm while Kade caught the man's shooting hand and bashed it against the floor.

Anthony cursed, but he still didn't stop fighting.

Neither did Bree or Kade. Bree rammed her elbow against Anthony's stomach, and he sputtered out a cough.

It was the break that Kade needed.

For just that split second, Anthony was distracted while he tried to catch his breath. Kade shoved Bree away from the man, and he brought down his fist into Anthony's jaw. His head flopped back.

And he dropped the gun.

Bree hurried to pick it up, and she put it right to Anthony's head.

"Give me a reason to kill you," she said. "Any reason will do."

Maybe she was bluffing, but after everything Anthony had put her through, maybe not.

Either way, Anthony believed her. He stopped struggling and his hands dropped limply by his sides.

Chapter Eighteen

"Can you drive any faster?" Kade asked his brother Nate.

It was exactly the question Bree had wanted to ask. She was more than grateful that Nate had stepped up to rush them to the Silver Creek hospital, but Bree wanted an emphasis on the *rush* part.

It was torture waiting to see their other daughter.

"I could drive faster," Nate drawled. "But I'd rather get there in one piece. Well, what's left of one piece. You do know you're both bleeding, right?"

Bree swiped at her lip again with the back of her hand. Yep. Still bleeding. She dabbed at the cut on Kade's forehead. She hated seeing the injuries there on his otherwise drop-dead gorgeous face, but the injuries were superficial and could wait. The baby couldn't. Well, she could, but Bree thought she might burst if she couldn't see her and make sure she was all right.

Nate's phone buzzed, and he answered it while he took the final turn to Silver Creek. The seconds and miles were just crawling by, even though it had only been twenty minutes or so since they'd left the Fulbright Clinic. When she'd looked back in the rearview mirror at the place, the SAPD officers had been stuffing a handcuffed Anthony McClendon into a patrol car.

Bree hoped he'd rot in jail.

It wasn't a forgive-and-forget sort of attitude to have, but she never wanted the man near her, Kade or their children again. Anthony was slime and had done everything in his power to destroy them.

Thank God, he hadn't succeeded.

"You're still bleeding," Kade let her know when she made another unsuccessful swipe at her mouth. He caught her chin, turned her head to face him and touched his fingers to her lip. "Does it hurt?"

She shook her head. There was probably pain, but she couldn't feel it right now. In fact, Bree couldn't feel much physically, only the concern she still had for Kade and their daughters.

"Does that hurt?" She glanced up at the bump and cut on his forehead.

"No." He kept his fingers on her mouth and his gaze connected with hers. He replaced his fingers with his lips and kissed her gently.

It stung a little, but Bree didn't care. The kiss warmed her and took away some of the ice that Anthony had put there. In fact, it even took some of the edge off her impatience and reminded her of something very important.

She smiled. "We won." With all the turmoil going on inside her and the hatred she had for Anthony, Bree hadn't had time to put things in perspective. Leave it to Kade's kiss to do exactly that. They'd won, and the prize was huge.

Kade smiled, too. "Yeah. And we're the parents of twin girls."

For just a moment that terrified her as she imagined trying to be a mother to both of them. *Twins.* Before Leah, she'd never even held a baby, and now she had two.

"You look like you're about to panic," Kade whispered.

Bree chuckled and winced as it pinched at her busted lip. "So do you."

He nodded. "Maybe a little. I'm thinking about how we can get through those 2:00 a.m. feedings with both of them."

"And the diapers." But suddenly that didn't seem so bad. It even seemed doable. Maybe because Kade had said *we*.

"You mean that?" Bree asked before she could stop herself.

He flexed his eyebrows and made a face from the tug it no doubt gave that knot on his head. "Mean what?"

Bree froze for a moment and considered, well, everything. Kade and she had known each other such a short time, and most of that time they'd been working undercover or getting shot at. Hardly the foundation for a relationship.

But somehow they'd managed just that—a relationship.

Of sorts.

Bree was still a little hazy on Kade's thoughts and feelings. However, hers were clearer now. Maybe because they'd come so close to dying tonight. That had certainly put things in perspective. So, she decided to go for it. She would question that *we,* and then she would tell him it was what she wanted, too. She wanted them to do this family thing together.

Whatever that entailed.

But before Bree could answer, Nate ended his call and looked back at them.

"They found Jamie's body," he let them know.

And just like that, Bree was pulled back into the

nightmarish memories that Anthony had given Kade and her. Enough nightmares to last a lifetime or two, and now Anthony had another victim—Jamie. Even though Bree didn't care for the woman's criminal activity, Jamie had tried to help her, and now she was dead because of it.

"Anthony confessed that he killed her," Kade explained.

"Yes, he confessed it to my men, too," Nate verified. "He'll be booked on capital murder changes, and he's not just looking at jail time but the death penalty."

Bree remembered something else he'd said. "Anthony murdered someone else. It's on the surveillance backups."

Nate nodded. "Kade gave them back to us, and we'll give them a thorough review. Trust me, we'll add any and all charges to make sure Anthony is never back on the streets again. His father, too, because Anthony said there'd be plenty enough on the backups to bring charges against Hector McClendon."

Good. After everything that had gone on at the clinic, McClendon certainly deserved to be punished.

Kade glanced at her first before looking at his brother. "Did Anthony say anything about Coop?"

"No, and from the sound of it, Anthony is blabbing about anyone who can be arrested for anything. A misery loves company sort of thing."

Bree felt the relief wash over her. So, her former boss and mentor wasn't dirty. That was something, at least, even though Kade's and her lives would never be the same.

And part of that wasn't all bad.

In fact, part of it was nothing short of a miracle. She might never have become a parent by choice, and it broke her heart to think of all the things she would have missed. She couldn't imagine life without Kade and the babies.

Except she might not have Kade.

And she didn't know what she would do if that happened.

Bree saw the Silver Creek hospital just ahead and knew her baby was inside. Just like that, the jitters and impatience returned with a vengeance. Her breath started to pound, her mouth went dry. She felt a little queasy.

And then Kade caught her hand in his and gave it a gentle squeeze. That squeeze was a reminder that she didn't want to do this alone.

No, that wasn't it.

She wanted to do this with Kade.

Bree looked at him to ask him about that *we* remark, but again she lost her chance when Nate stopped directly in front of the hospital doors. A discussion that would have to wait.

Kade and she barreled out, leaving Nate behind to park his SUV, and they rushed through the automatic doors. Her heart was in her throat by the time they made it to the lobby.

And then Bree saw them.

Mason was standing near the reception desk, and he was holding a baby who did indeed look exactly like Leah.

Kade's and her baby.

Bree knew that after just a glimpse.

The baby was crying, and Mason was trying to soothe her by rocking her. It wasn't working, and Mason looked more than a little uncomfortable with his baby-holding duties. Bree went to him, took the little girl and pulled her into her arms.

Yes, this child was theirs. Just holding her warmed every bit of Bree's heart.

Kade came closer, sliding his arm around both her and the baby. Leah's twin looked up at them as if trying to figure out if she was going to start crying again. She didn't. She just studied them.

Bree pulled back her blanket and studied her, too. Ten fingers, ten toes. There didn't appear to be a scratch on her, thank God.

"She's okay?" Bree asked Mason.

He nodded. "She's got a healthy set of lungs. And she peed on me." Mason frowned when he looked down at the wet spot on his shirt.

Bree smiled. Laughed. And then the tears came just as quickly. Her emotions were a mess right now, but the one thing she felt the most was the unconditional love. She pulled the baby closer and held on tight.

"It'll be okay," Kade whispered to her.

"Yes," Bree managed to say. "These are happy tears."

Kade smiled too. Kissed her, and then he kissed their daughter.

"The doc did a DNA test," Mason let them know. "But I don't think it's necessary."

"Neither do I," Kade agreed. "She's ours."

Behind them, the doors swished open, and because of the events of the night, Bree automatically pulled her daughter into a protective stance. Kade moved, too, to position himself in front of them.

But all their posturing wasn't necessary.

Grayson came through the doors, and he was carrying Leah in the crook of his arm. He stopped a moment, looking at the baby Bree was holding, and he smiled.

"Yeah, she's a Ryland all right." Grayson came closer and handed Leah to Kade.

"She's got a healthy set of lungs," Mason repeated in a mumble. He glanced at both babies. "Hope you don't expect me to babysit."

His tone was gruff, but Bree thought she saw the start of a smile. So this was what it felt like to be surrounded by family?

By love.

The *l*-word stopped her for a moment, and she looked up at Kade. No stop this time.

She was in love with him.

Bree wasn't sure why it'd taken her so long to come to that conclusion. It felt as if she'd loved him forever. Just like the babies.

Of course, that didn't mean he felt the same way about her. Yes, they had the twins, but that only meant they were parents. Not a couple in love. And it tore at her heart to realize she wanted it all, but she might not get it.

Kade might not love her.

"Why don't I get all you back to the ranch?" Grayson suggested. He gave the other twin's toes a jiggle. "What are you going to name her?"

"I've been calling her Mia," Mason volunteered and then looked uncomfortable with the admission. "Well, I had to call her something other than *kid,* and it rhymes with Leah."

Bree shrugged and looked up at Kade. He shrugged, too. "It works for me."

It worked for Bree, too.

So, they had Leah and Mia. The girls might hate the rhyming names when they got older, but they fit.

Everything about this moment fit.

Except for the person who came through the hospital doors.

Coop.

Everyone's attention went to him, and judging from Grayson's and Kade's scowls, they weren't any happier to see the man than she was. Bree wanted to spend this time with Kade and the girls. She definitely didn't want to go another round with her former boss.

"We were about to leave," Bree *greeted* him. And she hoped he understood there was nothing he had to say that she wanted to hear. She only wanted to leave.

Coop nodded. Glanced at the babies. There was no smile, only concern on his face. "I heard what happened, and I wanted to say how sorry I am."

There was no anger in his eyes or tone. The apology sounded heartfelt, and Bree was glad they were mending some fences, but her mind could hardly stay on the conversation.

"I came here to give you back your badge," Coop added. "I was wrong to put that kind of pressure on you."

"Yes, you were," Kade agreed.

Coop reached in his pocket and held out her badge.

Bree stared it a moment and then looked at each of her daughters. Then, at Kade. She had a decision to make and was surprised that it wasn't that hard to do.

"No, thanks," Bree said. And there wasn't a shred of doubt about this. "I can't go back to that life. It wouldn't give me much time for the girls."

Or Kade.

Coop's eyes widened. "You're serious?"

"Completely," she verified. "I want a job that'll keep me closer to Silver Creek."

Grayson shrugged. "I've got a deputy position open

in the Silver Creek sheriff's office. It's yours if you want it. After you've taken some maternity leave, that is."

Bree nodded and managed to whisper a thanks around the sudden lump in her throat. Later, she would tell him how much she appreciated that. The deputy position would keep her in law enforcement. And Silver Creek.

"But an FBI agent isn't just your job. It's who you are," Coop argued.

Bree looked him straight in the eye. "Not anymore. Goodbye, Coop."

Keeping a firm grip on the baby, Bree extended her hand for him to shake, but for a moment, she thought he might refuse. Finally, Coop accepted and shook her hand. He also hugged her.

"Have a good life, Bree." And he turned and walked back out.

Bree expected to feel some kind of pangs of... whatever, but she didn't. She looked up at Kade and didn't feel pangs there, either.

She just saw the man she loved.

Mason cleared his throat. "I'll bring the car to the door."

Grayson gave both Kade and her a look, too. "I'll help."

Clearly, Kade's brothers realized that this might become a private discussion. The *we* talk.

But Kade didn't exactly launch into a discussion. He leaned in and kissed her. Not a peck. A real kiss. It lasted so long that a nurse passing by cleared her throat.

Kade broke the intimate contact with a smile on his face. "No regrets about giving up your badge?"

"Not a one." And this was a do-or-die moment. A moment Bree couldn't let slip away again. "The only thing I regret is not telling you that I'm in love with you."

Kade froze in midkiss, and he eased back so they were eye to eye. Between them, both babies were wide-awake and playing footsies with each other. They both had their eyes fastened to their parents.

Then, Kade smiled. Really smiled. "Good." He hooked his left arm around Bree's waist and got as close to her as he could. "Because I'm in love with you, too."

Bree's breath vanished, and the relief she felt nearly brought her to her knees.

Kade was right there to catch her.

And kiss her.

This one melted her.

"Of course, that I-love-you comes with a marriage proposal," Kade said.

The melting turned to heat, and Bree wished they were somewhere private so she could haul him off to bed. Well, after the babies were asleep, anyway. She wasn't sure how they would work such things into their crazy schedule, but with this fierce attraction, they'd find a way.

Kade took Bree by her free hand. "Will you marry me, Bree?"

She didn't even have to think of her answer. "In a heartbeat."

·Kade let out a whoop that startled both babies and had several members of the hospital staff staring at them. Bree ignored the stares. Kissed both babies.

And then she kissed Kade.

She didn't stop until the babies' kicking became an issue, but Bree ended the kiss knowing there would be plenty of others in her future.

"Want to go home?" Kade asked.

Another easy answer. "Yes," she whispered.

Going home with Kade and their daughters was exactly what Bree wanted.

* * * * *

USA TODAY *bestselling author Delores Fossen's*
THE LAWMEN OF SILVER CREEK RANCH
miniseries continues next month with GAGE.
Look for it wherever
Harlequin Intrigue books are sold!

#1365 GAGE
The Lawmen of Silver Creek Ranch
Delores Fossen
After faking his death to protect his family, CIA agent Gage Ryland is forced to secretly return from the grave to save his ex, Lynette Herrington, who's carrying a secret of her own.

#1366 SECRET ASSIGNMENT
Cooper Security
Paula Graves
On a visit to a private island, an archivist stumbles onto an invasion, forcing her to work with the handsome caretaker to learn who will stop at nothing to gain access to the island—and why.

#1367 KANSAS CITY COWBOY
The Precinct: Task Force
Julie Miller
Sheriff Boone Harrison and police psychologist Kate Kilpatrick couldn't be more different. But trusting each other is the only way to catch a killer...and find a second chance at love.

#1368 MOMMY MIDWIFE
Cassie Miles
Nine months after a night she'll never forget, a pregnant midwife must trust the baby's father, a man she barely knows, to rescue her from the madman who wants her baby.

#1369 COPY THAT
HelenKay Dimon
A girl-next-door gets sucked into a dangerous new life when a wounded border patrol agent lands on her doorstep, with gunmen hot on his trail.

#1370 HER COWBOY AVENGER
Thriller
Kerry Connor
Her husband's murder turned her into an outcast and a suspect—and the only man who can help her is the tall, dark cowboy she thought she'd never see again.

REQUEST YOUR FREE BOOKS!
2 FREE NOVELS PLUS 2 FREE GIFTS!

Harlequin
INTRIGUE
BREATHTAKING ROMANTIC SUSPENSE

YES! Please send me 2 FREE Harlequin Intrigue® novels and my 2 FREE gifts (gifts are worth about $10). After receiving them, if I don't wish to receive any more books, I can return the shipping statement marked "cancel." If I don't cancel, I will receive 6 brand-new novels every month and be billed just $4.49 per book in the U.S. or $5.24 per book in Canada. That's a saving of at least 14% off the cover price! It's quite a bargain! Shipping and handling is just 50¢ per book in the U.S. and 75¢ per book in Canada.* I understand that accepting the 2 free books and gifts places me under no obligation to buy anything. I can always return a shipment and cancel at any time. Even if I never buy another book, the two free books and gifts are mine to keep forever.

182/382 HDN FEQ2

Name _____ (PLEASE PRINT)

Address _____ Apt. #

City _____ State/Prov. _____ Zip/Postal Code

Signature (if under 18, a parent or guardian must sign)

Mail to the **Reader Service:**
IN U.S.A.: P.O. Box 1867, Buffalo, NY 14240-1867
IN CANADA: P.O. Box 609, Fort Erie, Ontario L2A 5X3

Not valid for current subscribers to Harlequin Intrigue books.

**Are you a subscriber to Harlequin Intrigue books
and want to receive the larger-print edition?
Call 1-800-873-8635 or visit www.ReaderService.com.**

* Terms and prices subject to change without notice. Prices do not include applicable taxes. Sales tax applicable in N.Y. Canadian residents will be charged applicable taxes. Offer not valid in Quebec. This offer is limited to one order per household. All orders subject to credit approval. Credit or debit balances in a customer's account(s) may be offset by any other outstanding balance owed by or to the customer. Please allow 4 to 6 weeks for delivery. Offer available while quantities last.

Your Privacy—The Reader Service is committed to protecting your privacy. Our Privacy Policy is available online at www.ReaderService.com or upon request from the Reader Service.

We make a portion of our mailing list available to reputable third parties that offer products we believe may interest you. If you prefer that we not exchange your name with third parties, or if you wish to clarify or modify your communication preferences, please visit us at www.ReaderService.com/consumerschoice or write to us at Reader Service Preference Service, P.O. Box 9062, Buffalo, NY 14269. Include your complete name and address.

HII1B

ROMANTIC
SUSPENSE

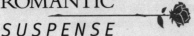

CINDY DEES

takes you on a wild journey to find the truth
in her new miniseries

Code X

Aiden McKay is more than just an ordinary man. As part of
an elite secret organization, Aiden was genetically enhanced
to increase his lung capacity and spend extended time under
water. He is a committed soldier, focused and dedicated
to his job. But when Aiden saves impulsive free spirit
Sunny Jordan from drowning she promptly overturns his
entire orderly, solitary world.

As the danger creeps closer, Adien soon realizes Sunny is the
target…but can he save her in time?

Breathless Encounter

Find out this August!

— *plus* —
**BONUS
STORY
INSIDE!**

www.Harlequin.com

HRS27786

Werewolf and elite U.S. Navy SEAL, Matt Parker, must set aside his prejudices and partner with beautiful Fae Sienna McClare to find a magic orb that threatens to expose the secret nature of his entire team.

Harlequin® Nocturne presents the debut of beloved author Bonnie Vanak's new miniseries, PHOENIX FORCE.

Enjoy a sneak preview of THE COVERT WOLF, available August 2012 from Harlequin® Nocturne.

Sienna McClare was Fae, accustomed to open air and fields. Not this boxy subway car.

As the oily smell of fear clogged her nostrils, she inhaled deeply, tried thinking of tall pines waving in the wind, the chatter of birds and a deer cropping grass. A wolf watching a deer, waiting. Prey. Images of fangs flashing, tearing, wet sounds...

No!

She fought the panic freezing her blood. And was gradually able to push the fear down into a dark spot deep inside her. The stench of Draicon werewolf clung to her like cheap perfume.

Sienna hated glamouring herself as a Draicon werewolf, but it was necessary if she was going to find the Orb of Light. Someone had stolen the Orb from her colony, the Los Lobos Fae. A Draicon who'd previously been seen in the area was suspected. Sienna had eagerly seized the chance to help when asked because finding it meant she would no longer be an outcast. The Fae had cast her out when she turned twenty-one because she was the bastard child of a sweet-faced Fae and a Draicon killer. But if she found the Orb, Sienna could return to the only home she'd known. It also meant she could recover her lost memories.

Every time she tried searching for her past, she met with a closed door. Who was she? Which side ruled her?

Fae or Draicon?

Draicon, no way in hell.

Sensing someone staring, she glanced up, saw a man across the aisle. He was heavily muscled and radiated power and confidence. Yet he also had the face of a gentle warrior. Sienna's breath caught. She felt a stir of sexual chemistry.

He was as lonely and grief stricken as she was. Her heart twisted. Who had hurt this man? She wanted to go to him, comfort him and ease his sorrow. Sienna smiled.

An odd connection flared between them. Sienna locked her gaze to his, desperately needing someone who understood.

Then her nostrils flared as she caught his scent. Hatred boiled to the surface. Not a man. Draicon.

The enemy.

Find out what happens next in THE COVERT WOLF by Bonnie Vanak.

Available August 2012 from Harlequin® Nocturne wherever books are sold.

Harlequin *Presents*

Discover an enchanting duet filled with glitz,
glamour and passionate love from

Melanie Milburne

THE *Outrageous* SISTERS

*The twin sisters **everyone's** talking about!*

Separated by secrets...

Having grown up in different families, Gisele and Sienna live lives
that are worlds apart. Then a very public revelation
propels them into the world's eye....

Drawn together by scandal!

Now the sisters have found each other—but are they at risk of losing
their hearts to the two men who are determined to peel back
the layers of their glittering facades?

Find out in

DESERVING OF HIS DIAMONDS?
Available July 24

ENEMIES AT THE ALTAR
Available August 21

www.Harlequin.com

HP89062